I take a deep breath (not that my lungs work, but old habits die hard) and enter the dining room, a wooden stake tip-down in each hand as I've been trained.

I edge the perimeter of the table, passing the first chair, the second.

So far so good.

The third.

Thwack!

As if attached to a cable, it shoves out and hits me square on the hip. (That's gonna leave a mark!)

The hooded figure arises from beneath the table.

I react immediately, shoving my stake dead center into its chest and recoiling as the hissing, burning, smoking robotic figure quakes before my very eyes.

I yank on my stake, desperate to get it back, but no luck. It's stuck for good.

That's the price you pay in Simulation House: stick a bloodsucker, lose your stake.

VAMPLAYERS

RUSTY FISCHER

VAMPLAYERS

MEDALLION
P R E S S
Medallion Press, Inc.
Printed in USA

Typeset in Adobe Garamond Pro
Printed in the United States of America

ISBN 978-1605424-49-1
10 9 8 7 6 5 4 3 2 1
First Edition

To Rhett, the ultimate Vamplayer (minus the V-A-M)!

PROLOGUE
fall 1981

It's daytime.

Why are they out in the daytime?

Rick Springfield is singing "Jessie's Girl," my favorite song of the moment.

I'm crooning into my hairbrush, kissing Rick's paper lips on his rockin' new poster hung crookedly on my peach-painted wall.

I pass my bedroom window, putting on a show for my imaginary audience of screaming, adoring fans outside when movement catches my eye. Lots of it.

People are on the front lawn outside my bedroom window, shadowy people with yellow eyes and long claws . . . and fangs?

But it's daytime.

How are they out in the daytime?

I should shut off my stereo, but it's my favorite part of the song. Besides, this must be a prank, right? The electricity goes out, cutting off the tune for me. *I wish that I had Jessie's gir—*

The figures are gone from the front lawn. See, some joke, huh?

My mom is in the kitchen whipping us up a quick midday snack, railing at the blender for cutting off midsmoothie. I see her standing there, still in her nurse's uniform and fresh from work, a run in her stockings. She gazes at the soupy mess in the blender, all red and pink and white and blotchy, then at me with those big green eyes. "Do you care if banana chunks are still in it?"

It's the last thing she'll ever say to me.

From the kitchen door a shadow passes across her. Only it's not a shadow; it's a man.

A Shadow Man.

Tall, lean, dressed all in black. Blood on his lips, on his dark-stubbled chin.

Bloodlust in his eyes.

He snags Mom's neck with long, white fangs

and slides them into her jugular like a warm knife through butter.

She never screams. Not once. It seems she was more upset when Dad left us than when this guy uses her throat like a toothpick.

I shriek at the first drop of blood on her starched white lapel and run back to my room, slamming the door, locking it tight, hunting for hiding places.

I ignore the space under my bed. Too obvious.

The closet? Even more obvious.

I open my hamper, a kind of wicker trash can, in the corner beside my desk.

It reeks of my cheerleading uniform from two days ago and that wet red towel I've been meaning to wash all week but never have. (Because I don't want my white panties to turn pink in case, you know, I let Randy Jenkins get to second base this weekend—or is it third? I dunno. I mean, which base involves panties?)

I stifle a gag, bury myself in warm, humid stank, and yank down the round lid, weak light filtering through.

I hear what must be Mom's body slumping to the hardwood kitchen floor, the blender shattering, Mom's almost rapturous sigh as the Shadow Man bites deep.

Eeww, Mom, gross.

There is a pause, a scraping, a gasp and now footsteps outside my room.

We have three doors in the hallway: Mom's bedroom; a spare room where she keeps her sewing machine to mend my cheer uniform, chorus gown, or last year's vampire Halloween costume (ironic much?); then there's my room.

I'm guessing that's Mom's door I hear exploding in a burst of wood and doorknob, clattering to the floor in a loud, scratchy heap. I cringe and burrow into the hamper, finding that gingham scarf I've been searching for since last week.

Metal hangers, apparently in Mom's walk-in closet, grate. A massive piece of furniture that must be her dresser crashes.

Footsteps in the hall again. Louder this time, getting closer, and I think it's more than one pair.

The sewing room is next, and they make quick work of it. I say *they* because it sounds like more than just the Shadow Man out there now.

I'm right. My door is next. After one or both of them kick it open, I hear four feet tromping across my floor.

I chew on my damp cheer sleeve to keep from

wailing. My heart is pounding; my palms are clammy; my legs are cramping from the awkward position I'm scrunched up in.

I hear the mattress get dragged off the frame and onto the floor, my closet doors tossed open. The sounds are violent, angry, powerful.

Boom!

Smash!

Crash!

The stomps advance, closer now. Drawers are jerked out of my desk before it topples over.

The hamper shakes, the top comes loose, but it's rolling on the floor toward the creamy peach wall, apparently unnoticed.

The heavy footsteps move toward my doorway, and I spill out, still covered in dirty clothes and non-pink panties.

I see the Shadow Man leading my mom (*Mom!*) out my door.

I stay perfectly still.

Mom stops, sniffs, pivots.

But it's not Mom I see. It's Monster Mom.

Vampire Mom.

Her neck is bloody. Her nursing uniform is splashed with red down the top left side. Her hair is askew, and her eyes are yellow and filled with a wild, hungry rage that seems to blot me out, paint a target on my throat, and draw her near. She spots me here beneath my brown and orange cheer skirt, a greedy smile slithering to her face. Light reflects off the drool streaming from the sharp, spiny tips.

Of.

My.

Mom's.

Fangs!

She doesn't say anything to the Shadow Man, only hisses him back with a gruff, almost animal language. The noise shatters the otherwise peaceful house, shakes the glass in my window.

The Shadow Man comes running, his footsteps pounding on the hollow wood floor.

I scramble to get up, the red towel, moist and moldy, wrapping around my legs, tripping me. I land with a thud on my bare wooden bed frame. It cracks; my arm smacks; the pain shoots through my elbow.

Mom sails across the room to me. Her fingernails, like claws, gouge at my skin.

"Mom. Mom! It's me, Lily, your daughter!"

She doesn't care, doesn't hear. Her mouth is a gaping maw of black and blood. With those awful,

glistening fangs, she tears at my skin.

The Shadow Man leans on the doorframe, laughing, licking his lips, letting Mom do the dirty work.

And it's so sunny out, the rays streaming through the windows. How is this happening now?

I pull back once, twice, straining my neck, yelping, my shoulders and arms growing slick with blood as Mom continues to scrape and scratch, seeking a hold on my neck.

We wrestle and grunt, the floor covered with gore. The last thing I see before Mom bites me is Rick Springfield staring down at me, black hair feathery, kind eyes sympathetic, shoulder muscles rippling just for me.

Now the ceiling shatters into a million pieces.

Men and women burst through and land on the floor.

I am spent, high and bleary like when my blood sugar gets too low and I'm about to pass out in fourth period before lunch.

A woman in a red leather jumpsuit aims a small crossbow at my mother's heart.

I want to warn the woman not to miss, not to screw it up.

She pulls the trigger.

Vampire Mom howls, shudders, sinks to the floor.

I join her, gurgling on my own blood, my head coming to rest on the stank red towel. I can feel the blood pumping from my jugular onto it, onto the floor, onto the bed frame.

Several red jumpsuits tackle the Shadow Man and fill him with short wooden stakes until his rib cage looks like a porcupine's backside.

The woman kneels at my side, her blonde hair in a simple ponytail, her blue eyes kind, her hands gentle. She presses gauze to my neck to stem the bleeding. Her full lips are moving. I strain to hear her and catch the end: ". . . old are you?"

"Seventeen." I cough up blood and start to pass out. The sunlight streams in, and Rick gazes at me, not quite smiling, not quite frowning, all kinds of sexy in his white tank top.

"Good," I hear her saying, or at least I think I do, as my eyes shut. "We need another Sister."

All is black, no more sunlight, no more Vampire Mom, no more Springfield.

My last words are, "I don't have any sisters."

A voice, close enough to stir my long black hair, says softly, "You do now."

CHAPTER 1

I enter the house on cat's feet. No, scratch that. Rewind. Cats don't have feet, do they? Paws, right? So I enter the house on cat's paws. No, that's not right either, because I'm kind of just on my toes, not my whole feet, and who walks on their toes? Okay, I enter the house on ballerina's feet (there, that's better!) and quietly shut the door.

The home is silent and dim, but I don't reach for the lights. I don't have to. My vampire vision illuminates the scene in that old familiar yellow glow, as if candles flicker all around. They don't.

I take my time in the foyer getting my bearings, though I've been here literally hundreds of times

9

before. Still, every time is different. The Academy makes sure of that.

The foyer is easy to inspect. It's about the size of a closet, no windows, just the front door and a neat little end table featuring a potted plant and glazed ceramic bowl with a house key inside.

I check it off mentally and move forward, creeping into the living room on my ballerina toes.

But show me the ballerina who skulks around in thick-soled black sneakers with matching socks, yoga pants, and hoodie, and I'll show you a dancer starring in a really, really off-Broadway *Black Belt Swan*.

The living room is straight out of the seventies with ugly boxy leather sofas the color of week-old peas and an orange recliner featuring a mushroom throw pillow that's seen better days. The detail is pretty amazing, down to the cheesy cork coasters and outdated, dusty *LIFE* magazines on the kidney-shaped coffee table.

But I'm not here for the nickel tour.

I'm here to do one thing and one thing only: survive.

The house is still, no signs of ferocious blood-suckers. Yet.

The living room is bigger, more corners to

search, more nooks and crannies to hide in, and of course more potential for bloody booby traps.

I tiptoe, alert for sudden movement or anything out of the ordinary. You know, like roving bands of the undead wearing sideburns and dressed in seventies seersucker suits. All the while my toes feel for tiny pressure changes on the orange shag carpeted floor, which would mean I've tripped a trigger and a shiny, stainless steel stake is now headed for my heart.

Nothing behind the couch, the love seat, or the curtains covering windows shuttered against the fake sun. I clear the living room without incident. That is, if you consider a pounding stress headache crushing my cranium a nonincident.

I stand at the threshold of the dining room. Now, if the living room is a playground of dangerous nooks and crannies designed to trip me up, then the dining room is an obstacle course of potentially deadly booby traps designed to bring me down: big, long dinner table, six straight-back chairs, framed clown art on the walls (now *that's* spooky), more fake windows, more dense, dangling drapes.

You could spend hours in here searching every hidey-hole and cranny-nook, but I have only twenty minutes to clear the entire house, and there are still three rooms plus one particularly nasty staircase left if I'm to complete my assignment on time.

Cue the *Mission: Impossible* theme.

I take a deep breath (not that my lungs work, but old habits die hard) and enter the dining room, a wooden stake tip-down in each hand as I've been trained.

I edge the perimeter of the table, passing the first chair, the second.

So far so good.

The third.

Thwack!

As if attached to a cable, it shoves out and hits me square on the hip. (That's gonna leave a mark!)

The hooded figure arises from beneath the table.

I react immediately, shoving my stake dead center into its chest and recoiling as the hissing, burning, smoking robotic figure quakes before my very eyes.

I yank on my stake, desperate to get it back, but no luck. It's stuck for good.

That's the price you pay in Simulation House: stick a bloodsucker, lose your stake.

Oh well, best to move along.

The close call only makes me more alert. I clear the dining room quickly, decisively, managing to avoid any more surprises or tripped booby traps along the way.

Out in the hall, staring up the fourteen steps to the second story, I sigh and take each one slowly.

They are wood, and each one creaks. I'm half-way up when the first pressure point hisses.

I duck immediately, just missing being impaled by the stake that flies past my raven ponytail.

There's nothing left to do but run straight up, taking the steps two at a time. The stakes shoot out so fast, so often that they create a steady breeze between my legs as they slam into the opposite wall with a pistonlike thump-thwack-splat, spreading drywall chunks and asbestos dust through the air.

I make it to the landing at the top of the stairs, but there's still no relief. I've wasted ten minutes downstairs and still have three rooms to clear up here.

And now it gets *really* tricky.

First up is the bathroom, another simple room with only one place for the bad, if fake, vampires to hide: behind the powder-blue vinyl shower curtain. But every tile on the way there is a potential stake in my foot. Not quite deadly, but it wouldn't exactly tickle either.

Instead of taking another step inside the room, I carefully open the cabinet under the sink, pull out a plunger (I told you the attention to detail in this place is incredible!), and toss it at the shower curtain.

I duck immediately, and it's a good thing.

One, two, three stakes puff out through the tattered curtain, piercing the wall above and slightly to the left of my head.

I have to waste two precious minutes freeing my ponytail from one of the skewers. (Hey, just because I'm a bloodsucker doesn't mean I don't care about my hair.)

I turn from the room, clear the guest bedroom in less than a minute, and step tentatively toward the next obstacle.

Ah, the master bedroom, where I lose it every.

Single.

Time.

The door is already open, and I stride through purposefully. The big digital clock over the gold lamé curtains tells me I have only three minutes and forty-six seconds to complete my mission.

I shake my head, putting sneakers to the turquoise shag rug, and quickly secure the bed, over and under, even the closet with twelve hangers full of dusty Goodwill suits nobody will ever wear again.

I pivot and realize I never cleared the front door.

A simple hiss kills me in my tracks.

The stake hits the thin black titanium breastplate covering my chest, bouncing off harmlessly but triggering a hidden sensor that instantly floods the bedroom in light, sets off a blinking, rotating siren on the bedroom ceiling (the kind you used to see on old cop cars), and quickly ends my quest to become Afterlife Academy's next Savior.

The curtains on both sides of me pull back immediately: one to reveal the school's sexy headmistress, Dr. Haskins, the other to display her large but simple and well-lit office.

Dr. Haskins doesn't look like a regular doctor but more like a soap opera doctor, with her long blonde hair in an updo, black chopsticks holding it in place, her rectangular glasses black and sleek in front of her deep blue eyes, her lips red and thick, and her shimmering silver jacket open and just barely covering a likewise revealing white silk blouse.

Her short gray skirt whispers as she crosses the room on long legs, her black heels clunky but fashionable. In her hand is her ever present clipboard, which she is currently ticking off fast and furious.

"Lily, Lily, Lily," she says, voice officious and clipped. She stops to stand in front of me. She's about five feet eight but still has to look up to school me (okay, only an inch or two, but still). "What did I tell you about clearing the front door first, not last?"

"I know, I know." I'm aware my whiny voice is pitiful but can't stop myself. "I guess I saw how little time I had left and just panicked."

She hears me out, then scribbles something incriminating (probably) on her Lucite clipboard. "The best way to add more time on the back end of your Simulation is to take less time at the front."

I nod, biting my lip helplessly.

She takes a step out of the simulated bedroom and the clear door to her office slides open automatically.

I follow her inside.

The guts of her office are all shimmery and shiny and absolutely see-through, like something Willy Wonka might design for his chocolate factory. She has clear furnishings: desk, chair, and filing cabinets. I wonder for the first time if her employee bathroom has a clear toilet. I'll have to ask the other Sisters when my evaluation is over.

"I'm sorry." She extends a hand across the desk.

I unstrap the light but awkward Simulation Shield from around my chest and hand it over.

"I can't pass you this time. I'm certain you understand."

I make a clicking sound with my tongue. "No, frankly I don't understand. How many times can I run the Simulation before we both say enough is enough? I mean, how can I be good enough to be a Sister but not good enough to be a Savior? I just don't understand."

"No," she says, sounding severe. "You *don't* understand. Being a Sister is about preventing infestations. Being a Savior is about stopping them once they've started. It's an entirely different psychology, and mastering this Simulation is your first step toward mastering the psychology."

Oh great. Now in addition to kicking butt and taking names, I have to be a psychologist. I slump in my clear plastic seat, wondering what my butt looks like from beneath. *Stop, Lily. Focus.* "This bites."

She finally sighs, licking the thick lips that hide her veteran fangs. "Metaphorically speaking, of course." She smiles.

I almost smile, to be polite, but it stops halfway to my lips.

She sets down the clipboard, pushes herself back just a smidge from her big, intimidating desk, and crosses those long, luxurious legs. "You know I have nothing but respect for you and the other

Sisters. But I'm sensing a certain, shall we say, reluctance to pass this Simulation. It's like, I don't know, all three of you are afraid to take the next step. As you know, there is no place for fear as a Savior."

"How can you say that?" I whine. "Every month we get dropped into some new high school and have to sniff out some dirty, sneaky, dangerous Vamplayer. Once he finds out our true identity, we have to battle him and anyone he may have turned. It's *exactly* like being a Savior."

She shakes her head firmly. "That's where you're wrong, Lily. It's but a *taste* of being a Savior. That's all this Simulation is as well: a small taste."

I let her words sink in.

Could she be right?

Are Cara, Alice, and I too comfortable as Sisters to ever be Saviors? But how can that be when all we want is to wear those hip-hugging leather jumpsuits and carry around personal-sized crossbows?

Dr. Haskins stands, signaling the abrupt end of our meeting.

"I'm sorry." I sigh, just like I have after failing the Simulation countless times before. "I'll try harder next time. I promise."

"I have no doubt you will. But Saviors don't try, Lily. They do. They don't promise. They achieve. Think about that as you train this week, and you'll be better prepared when next we meet."

CHAPTER 2

"Okay, seriously, this place now officially sucks." Alice pushes away her plate of sautéed blood clots, her pale and pristine face a not-so-subtle mask of disgust. "Why ask me how I want them prepared if you're going to overcook them anyway?"

From across the table for four, Cara shoots me a *here we go again* look.

I bite back a smile. "Why don't you take them back if you don't like them?"

Alice sighs loudly, preferring to suffer out loud rather than be happy in silence. "No. They might spit in my food for spite."

Cara and I snicker.

I scoop up the last of my blood consommé, my spoon clinking against the nearly empty bowl.

Cara wraps her long, mocha-colored fingers around her plastic tumbler and finishes off the last of her type B smoothie. She smacks her lips and sets the empty cup on the faux wood cafeteria table. "My lunch was absolutely fantastic, as usual."

Alice looks at Cara's empty plate. "Well, anyone who shoves down their blood clots any old way hardly has a discriminating palate."

Cara slides a thin cornrow behind her ear and glares at Alice. "Who are you discriminating against now, Alice?"

"W-what? Who, me? Nobody. Wait, what?"

Cara smiles.

I tidy my tray and watch the would-be Saviors slowly leaving the cafeteria in their tight little groups.

They ignore us for the most part, like seniors with freshmen, lettermen with geeks, hot girls with chicks in Weight Watchers.

I watch them saunter, laughing, big and strong, vampires through and through, off to another aikido or judo or fencing class, off to study the grand vampiric languages or the history of Transylvania, off to save lives, chew gum, and kick some bloodsucking booty.

I frown, thinking of Dr. Haskins and her theory that the girls and I are just too comfortable being Sisters trapped in high school forever to ever be Saviors on our own.

I can't believe that. I *refuse* to believe that. I mean, everyone at the Academy wants to be a Savior. That's why we're here in the first place.

The Saviors are, in a word, badass. When a city gets infested—when the cops, the feds, even the army can't handle it—who do they call? The Saviors. When one, two, or three hundred screaming vampires rampage a town looking for fresh victims in the middle of the street, who do they call? The Saviors.

Like some kind of vampire superheroes on steroids, they swoop into town wearing their red leather jumpsuits and sleek motorcycle boots, wielding their monogrammed stakes and personal-sized crossbows, cutting down vampires left and right.

Who wouldn't want to do that for a living, right?

And what do we do? The Sisterhood of Dangerous Girlfriends? We get dropped into schools where officials or the occasional anonymous tipster suspect a verifiable vampire sighting. We rout him out, identify the girl he's trying to neck with (literally), become her girlfriends, and stop an infestation before it happens.

Bor-ing.

And not just boring but seriously?

High school?

In the six years I've been a Sister, I have lived in nearly every state and attended over seventy high schools.

It. Is. Terrifying.

Imagine being trapped in high school.

For.

Ev.

Er.

Just . . . gross.

It's like that ancient Greek myth, the one about the guy who tricked the gods into letting him out of the underworld, then refused to go back. You know, Sisyphus, or what's his name? And as punishment they sentenced him to roll a great big rock up a hill every day only for it to roll down just before he reached the top so that the next day he had to roll it right back up. For eternity.

Except our ball is a great big spit wad.

So Dr. Haskins is wrong.

I don't want to stay a Sister forever. Nobody does.

I *do* want to be a Savior. In the worst possible way. I just haven't gotten the hang of Simulation

House ye—

The cafeteria is silent, which means one of two things. Either Alice and Cara have left the building (because, seriously, those two never stop talking) or they *have* stopped talking, if only momentarily, and they're waiting for me to answer a question so they can go back to talking as soon as I open my mouth.

I look up and see their mouths shut, their eyes staring at me expectantly.

We're alone now. The cafeteria is completely and suddenly empty. "Huh? What? Why? How? *When?*"

Cara smiles. "Why so down, Lily?"

I shrug.

Alice figures it out right away. "She had her Simulation today. It must not have gone very well, huh?" She tries to hide her pretty obvious pleasure at my misfortune, but we all know Alice loves being First Sister and hates the thought of giving up her title. As Third Sister, I'm no direct threat to her—yet.

And that's exactly how she likes to keep it.

"Not really," I grumble.

Cara reaches across the table and pats the top of my hand. "Let me guess: the bedroom tripped you up again?"

I nod. "I just don't get it. I mean, how many

times have we trained, all of us, to clear the bedroom door first? And every time I forget."

Cara frowns, pulling her hand away to stack dishes on her tray. "I don't think Dr. Haskins wants us to pass the Simulation."

Alice groans.

Cara goes on. "Think about it. If we move up to Savior status, where will Dr. Haskins find some new Sisters? You know nobody here respects us, so why would they want to *be* us?"

Alice shrugs. "You could have a point." She snaps her collar. "We are pretty badass. Am I right?"

We high-five, but my heart's not in it.

"What does that mean then?" I say. "We're doomed to be Sisters forever?"

"Dang," Alice says, leaning back in her chair. "I thought you enjoyed our company. Would it be that bad hanging with us forever? Even if it does mean being Third Sister for all eternity?"

I smirk.

She smirks.

We get it, Alice. We get it: you're First Sister.

"It's not you I want to get away from," I kinda lie. "When I started this job, I thought it would be temporary, you know? 'It's only for a year or two,

Lily.' That's what Dr. Haskins told me on my first day, remember? And now, six years and who knows how many schools later, I'm no closer to being a Savior."

"I know I'm ready to move up." Cara rubs her hands against her narrow, tapered waist. "Not for nothin', but this body was made for one of those red leather jumpsuits, feel me?"

We share a laugh, even Alice, who would be the first to dive into a pool full of holy water if Cara ever became First Sister.

I smile, picturing Cara, Alice, all of us in matching jumpsuits, those precious crossbows dangling from our black leather belts.

We grow silent, strutting through the halls in our fantasies, until Alice says, "What's a few more years of being a Sister anyway, Lily? Look how long it took you to become a Sister. Twentysomething years? That's got to be some kind of record."

"Hush, Alice," Cara says, offering me a sympathetic look.

But it's nothing I haven't heard before. "So I'm a slow learner. What can I say? I mean, it's not like—" My pager goes off, and I groan.

Cara and Alice instinctively flinch as their pagers go off as well.

We look at each other before quickly cleaning up our trays.

Pagers can mean only one thing: a new assignment.

If only I'd held on to one of those stakes from my Simulation, I'd impale myself right now.

CHAPTER 3

Cara and I stand apprehensively at the door to our dorm suite, but Alice is absolutely brimming with excitement.

She rushes ahead of us to open the door as if she might find a fully decked out Christmas tree and dozens of presents waiting. "Finding out where we're going is the best part, you guys," she says cheerleader-style and dashes into the room first. She grabs the leather dossier resting just so on our coffee table.

"Am I the only one who thinks it's creepy the way they always deliver those things while we're out of the room?" I say.

"What?" Alice flops onto the couch and luxuriates

in opening the file first. "Would you rather they hunt us down in the cafeteria and hand it over in front of all those would-be Saviors?"

"I guess not."

It's not that I'm embarrassed to be a Sister, let alone Third Sister, ie the puniest, least respected student on campus. It's just that everyone at the Academy treats us differently.

Like when we get an assignment, it's all cloaks and daggers, hush-hush, super spy Jason Bourne stuff, you know? All of a sudden, without any warning, someone drops off a file in our room and we pack up and ship out without any fanfare or hoopla.

But when the Saviors get sent out on a mission, look out! It's all bells and whistles and practically a ticker tape parade. Most of the school empties out to watch the elite of the elite get into their rock star tour bus and head off to parts unknown.

Cara hauls out her old-school, faded army-green duffel bag and fills it with panties and bras.

"Has anyone seen my curling iron?" Annoyed, I stare daggers at Alice, who buries her nose in the dull-as-dirt dossier.

I stalk into her room, and on her cluttered vanity is the evidence—still plugged in!

I unplug it and scan Alice's room while I wait for it to cool off. This girl is whack, seriously, end of story. Although it's strictly forbidden and against all kinds of Academy protocol to bring souvenirs from any of our assignments, Alice's room is crammed full of knickknacks, pennants, ribbons, and trophies from her years of endless high school exploits. I guess rank does have its privileges after all.

Then there are the yearbooks lined row after row in three custom bookshelves across from her bed, one for each of her nearly three hundred assignments by now. One more reason Alice is so proud to be First Sister: she's been doing it decades longer than I have.

The yearbooks date back to the early seventies, when Dr. Haskins herself started the Sisterhood; hence, the retro Simulation House, which has never been updated. She wasn't a doctor back then, of course, but since it was her idea to start the Sisterhood and the program has been so successful, Dr. Haskins was given opportunities to rise through the ranks and, eventually, headmistress status at the Academy.

I pick up a yearbook, open it to a random page, and see Alice's loopy handwriting circling an awkward-looking boy with a feathery eighties haircut.

She's written *Super Dreamy* in a bubble around his head.

I groan, grab the warm curling iron, and pack it in my bag.

At my closet, I look for my favorite gray scarf. "Uh, Cara?" I knock on her doorjamb.

There's no need. She holds out the scarf, head down, murmuring apologies, and shoves another pair of yoga pants deep into her skuzzy green duffel.

"Thanks," I say, wrapping it around my throat dramatically. "Why do you use that ratty old thing? You know you get an expense account on each assignment. Surely you've saved enough to buy a few dozen designer bags by now."

She looks at the bag ruefully. "I know, but this was my dad's before the infestation that . . . ended him. When the Saviors came and found me, I packed up some stuff in this. It's all I have left, you know? Of him."

I try to hug her.

She smiles instead, shrugging off my display of emotion. "I'm fine, girl. That was ages ago. I'm over it."

Ah, but we're never really over it, are we?

I pretend to buy the lie because it's easier—for her—and stare at her clean yellow walls covered in framed prints of pristine cottages, herb gardens, and white picket fences. Cara's dream: the simple, non-vampire, non-Sister life.

I look at the single bed, cozy white comforter, floral throw pillows, her hat rack in the corner holding Easter Sunday straw hats from her childhood (when church services and crosses didn't make her skin actually boil), and scarves, most of them mine.

I smile and return to my room. It's bare by comparison, almost sterile. It used to be covered with old eighties posters, things from before I became a vampire and after. Things that made me feel human and alive and reminded me of a simpler, more innocent time.

I would have brought the posters from my own walls, the ones I stared at every night before bed and every morning while I was getting ready for school, but when the Saviors came to rescue me that day, they weren't exactly worried about saving my posters. Just my hide.

I bought them online at some great retro sites using my Academy expense accounts: old Rick Springfield and *The Breakfast Club* posters, album covers from the Go-Go's and Madonna ("Like a Virgin" era). But I took them all down years ago.

When you become a Savior, they move you to

the single dorms. No sharing a bathroom, no one borrowing your scarves or curling irons and never returning them.

Every Simulation Day I expect to come back to my room, grab my bags, and stroll on over to the Savior side of the dorms, never looking back. It hasn't quite worked out that way.

I've had bare walls for two years. I'm thinking maybe it's time to unroll Rick Springfield again. If I can't even make it through Simulation House after all this time, I might be here awhile.

"Ooohh," Alice says from the living room, nose still in the leather dossier. "Check it out, kiddies. We're headed to scenic Ravens Roost, North Carolina, and a joint called the Nightshade Conservatory for Exceptional Boys and Girls."

"That doesn't sound right." Cara abandons her packing to log on to our standard-issue circa 1992 computer. "Do they mean, like, short bus exceptional or gifted exceptional?"

"I can't imagine Vamplayers going anywhere the kids aren't picture perfect, you know?" I walk toward Cara to look at the screen.

She pulls up Nightshade Conservatory's official website. "Ooohh, ritzy."

That finally draws Alice from the couch.

Cara clicks on pictures of an old-school, castle-style campus with manicured grounds and great, high towers dotted with ornate stained glass windows and spooky gargoyles.

"Now that," Alice says dreamily at my side, "looks like just the kind of place a Vamplayer would find attractive. And the kind of place where pretty, pretty boys flirt with pretty, pretty girls." She does a little dance.

I see her in my periphery but refuse to acknowledge her.

"See if they have any photo galleries of the sports team," she says. "I need to know if I should pack slutty or, you know, extra slutty."

"Extra slutty," Cara and I answer in unison.

"Hey," she says, walking away to do just that.

Cara logs off, and we settle into the grim, dull routine of packing for our next assignment.

CHAPTER 4

The private jet lands on a small airstrip high in the mountains. A gloomy mist greets us as the fiftysomething pilot opens the door and helps the four of us down to the gray tarmac.

Dr. Haskins exits last, her crisp khaki traveling suit snug but not too seductive. She clutches a single matching handbag. She won't be staying long. She never does.

A limo meets us beyond the airstrip. By the time our luggage is stowed and we're all settled in the backseat, the tiny jet has already been refueled and turned around and awaits Dr. Haskins' imminent return.

The drive to the Nightshade Conservatory for

Exceptional Boys and Girls is winding and steep and lined with little except trees, boulders, and more trees.

"Hmm," Alice says as we pass a small town nestled in the hills, "guess we won't be sneaking out of our dorms too often around this dump."

Dr. Haskins presses a small button to raise the soundproof divider between the backseat and the driver. "Alice makes a good point, girls."

"She does?" Cara and I ask.

I'm dumbfounded.

Even Alice seems surprised. "I do?"

"Well, in a roundabout way, of course. Nightshade is extremely secluded. This road is the only way up or down. That town we passed is the last one for miles. Ten of them, to be exact. It's called Ravens Roost, and about twelve hundred people live there, whose sole job is to serve and staff the Conservatory." She gives us a look like it's our fault the town decided to build itself halfway up a mountain in the middle of nowhere.

"The nearest hospital is twenty miles away at the bottom of the mountain. The nearest police precinct is five miles south of that. I don't have to tell you that if an infestation started at the school, there would be little chance of stopping it before it affected all five hundred eighty students, one hundred forty-seven staff, and of course the good people of Ravens Roost. So we can't have any screw-ups this time." She looks at Alice purposefully before concluding, "And you have to sniff out the Vamplayer and stop him in his tracks before he turns a single student. Do I make myself clear?"

We nod, as we always do. We've heard this speech once or twice before.

"Who reported it?" Cara says, hands folded primly on her knees.

"Nobody. Our Information Gatherers have reported a dozen mysterious deaths in Ravens Roost in the last few weeks—farm animals mostly, a few family pets—but a local veterinarian grew suspicious and started logging in to one of those *I Think We Have a Vampire in Our Midst* blogs. You know we monitor all those. He and several hundred residents of Ravens Roost have filed formal complaints about the students of Nightshade, claiming they saw a mysterious figure appearing from the mountain about the time of the attacks and returning to Nightshade afterward. The Council of Ancients decreed we should run a mission, see if there's anything to it."

I tap the dossier on my lap. "There was no list of recent student admissions."

She purses her lips and shakes her head. "Highly unusual, I know, but since Nightshade is private, I couldn't locate the public records for new transfers. The headmistress wasn't very . . . forthcoming, to say the least. I'm sorry. If anyone can sniff out the Vamplayer, it's you girls."

Her smile seems fake and insincere. Meanwhile, as our car climbs toward Nightshade, the mood in the car remains somber. And why shouldn't it?

It's a lot of pressure being one of only three girls responsible for nearly two thousand mortals and stopping a Vampire Armageddon, but it's certainly nothing we haven't faced or won't again. I'm not sure why I'm so anxious this time, except that I was hoping to be a Savior by now.

Oh well, maybe next eternity.

The drive evens out to a more gradual climb, and soon I hear pavement instead of gravel beneath the tires. Outside the deeply tinted windows is a large stone fence that seems to circle the entire property. Beyond the fence are miles and miles of dense, tall forest. Within are a pristine lawn and the typical markings of a modern-day private academy: rugby and soccer fields, a basketball half-court, a full track, small sitting areas, a large paved quad with a fountain in the middle and natural stone benches all around.

As we approach the entrance, an old metal gate swings open with a yawning screech that seems fitting for such a gloomy, austere environment. It's mid-October, but the manicured trees lining the drive to the Nightshade Admissions Office are not gloriously covered in autumn colors. They're already stripped and bare, kind of like my hopes of being a Savior by now.

Alice's eyes are wide, her tongue slightly out, as she observes the enormity of the school. It's like she's never done this before.

Ever the honor student, Cara is already scribbling in a little black notebook.

I peek at her sketch of the front gate, then sit back to enjoy the show. After all, when you're Third Sister, nobody expects much of you.

The car stops.

Before we get out, Dr. Haskins opens her fist.

Inside are three small gadgets, charcoal-colored and no bigger than credit cards. Each has a small red button on top next to a thin LED screen.

"Here are your pagers," she says. "Same drill as always: they work once and only once and in one direction: straight to my office. Use them in case of extreme emergency, and remember it will take a full team of Saviors at least four hours to get here, so handle them wisely and, if you use them at all, use them early."

We take the pagers, secret them into our bags, and hope it doesn't come to that.

Knock on coffin wood, I haven't had to use mine all year.

Then again, there's always a first time.

As if on cue, the driver opens the door and escorts each of us onto a paver-lined parking circle.

Dozens of windows gleam from within the gray stone walls of Nightshade. I don't look up to make sure, but I feel hundreds of pairs of eyes checking us out as we walk slowly up four large, granite steps to a massive stone entryway. It's like the feeling you get when someone reads over your shoulder in the subway.

Cara leans in and whispers, "I thought *we* were supposed to be the spooky ones."

I stifle a snort.

Dr. Haskins cuts me a look as we follow her through the front door and into the grand entrance.

The school's headmistress waits for us, smiling. A refreshingly young woman, she sports a suit snug enough to give Dr. Haskins a run for her money. She stands next to a large, round oak table that holds a vase of breathtaking fresh flowers.

The foyer is massive, as big as Simulation House itself. Its floors are marble. Its granite walls are lined with banners, most as big as movie screens and hanging from long metal rods with gold tassels on the ends, depicting old English hunting scenes: foxes, beagles, white horses, and men in red jackets.

Beyond the foyer I hear the typical high school sounds: lockers slamming, shoes squeaking, laughter, conversation, a book dropped, papers rustling, someone shouting playfully, "Give it back, Rufus!"

The two women give each other a quick, pumping power shake. No hugs for these two.

Dr. Haskins introduces each of us.

Headmistress Holly smiles but does not shake our hands. "Ladies," she says, though mostly to Dr. Haskins, "follow me." She turns on her heel and marches down a marble hallway, her shoes clacking endlessly through the twists and turns.

I glimpse a few students on our journey, probably student aides since we seem to be in some kind of

administrative wing. There is no uniform at Nightshade, and in fact the kids we see look like any kids
we've ever seen anywhere: pale and hungry, long and
limber, wary and whispering of "the new kids."

I resist the temptation to wave. Alice's voice echoes
in my mind from a dozen missions or more: *You're too
nice, Lily. That's why you're the Third Sister. Don't even
smile until week two; everybody knows that!* I can't help
it. Her advice makes me smile all the more.

We stop at a huge wooden door with a pointy
top and two big, black metal bands about halfway
up. Its iron handle is long and thin, like in some old
medieval castle.

The headmistress opens it and ushers us in.

For a room with such a big door, her office is
surprisingly small.

The two grown-ups stand and smile, then sit
across from each other, a tidy desk between them.

We Sisters stand awkwardly aloof in the back as
the two headmistresses make polite chitchat ("How
was your flight?" "I love that scarf").

I check out the walls. They are full of the obliga-
tory diplomas and credentials plus a handful of
framed glossies of pretty Headmistress Holly shaking
hands with local politicians and a few old celebrities.

A barred window to my right overlooks a solemn courtyard. Movement below captures my attention. I move closer, trying not to be too obvious.

A tall, striking young man with long black hair and a black trench coat lights a cigarette.

I smile. All kids everywhere are the same. Iron gates, early curfews, and efficient headmistresses can't keep them from lighting up whenever they get the chance.

He does it pretty cavalierly for a student, though, not even bothering to see if anyone's looking.

Someone is.

A figure with a luxurious auburn mane slinks into view. She's dressed in black leggings and a black thigh-length sweater that hugs every curve (she's got plenty). A gray scarf is wound around her elegant neck.

Though they stand apart and never once touch, the two look intimate. I watch smoke ooze from his mouth as he speaks.

Maybe that's why she stands just a little too far away. I know I would.

They smile often, though, and their body language implies intimacy either already shared or about to be any damn moment.

With his large, pale hands, he tosses away one

cigarette and immediately lights another. He offers it to her.

She demurs.

He laughs, smoke rising from his open lips.

She slaps his shoulder playfully.

Of course, there is nothing particularly menacing about a drop-dead handsome guy smoking in a courtyard with a beautiful girl, but something about this guy stands out as vaguely, well, vampirific.

Here's the thing about the Vamplayers we Sisters hunt down: they're cool.

And not only in a jock, hot, player, rich, funny, or smart kind of way.

They are beyond cool.

You know high school guys, right? They're basically all the same. Some are cuter than others, some taller, some shorter, some better dressed, some less so. But the cool ones are always still just high school cool. Maybe you don't know it until you graduate or he dumps you and starts dating your best friend or you see him drunk for the first time or he gets too grabby at a keg party and then lies about you to all his friends the next morning—but high school cool is not the same as cool-cool, you know?

This guy is cool-cool. Adult cool, movie star

cool, rich cool, don't-care-anymore cool.

He's not looking to impress friends or score another chick or carve another notch on his belt or hook up or break up. He looks like he's been there done that three thousand times before.

This kind of cool is not one thing you can point to and say, "See that right there? That's what I mean."

It's two dozen things.

Like the way smoke curls out of his thin, pink lips and into his streamlined, almost royal nostrils. Like the way he lazily reaches out and whisks a snaking tendril of sleek auburn hair off the girl's cheek. Like the way he laughs, not rushed, nowhere to be but right here right now with this girl, smoking this cigarette.

Like the way he stands tall while she moves around, slouching, cocking her head, jutting out her breasts then reeling them in, as if she's still trying to read his signals when he's already had hers figured out for weeks, even if they've just met. Like the way he leans against the short stone wall as if it was built just for him. Like the way his eyes stay focused on her even when a squirrel scampers past and she points excitedly and laughs, her hand covering her mouth.

In short, he's not just high school cool. He's vampire cool.

I try to alert Cara to a potential Vamplayer sighting, but she's listening intently to something Headmistress Holly is saying.

By the time I peer out the window again, the girl is gone. I look left, right, curious where she's gone and why and how they ended it and if they kissed or fought or if she simply walked away while he barely raised a hand in good-bye (if that).

The boy isn't gone.

He's staring at me, smoke curling around his nostrils as he opens his mouth to give me a wide smile that says, *Well, hello there. Hmm, how long have you been standing there? Hey, you don't look all that bad yourself.*

Great. It's like the master bedroom in the Simulation House all over again. Five minutes on the job, and I'm already tipping my hand.

I move away from the window and give my full attention to the headmistress, trying to shake the too-cool-for-school guy out of my brain and concentrate.

". . . late in the year for one, let alone three, students to apply. You'll understand my concern, Dr. Haskins."

"Of course." She has heard it all before and, thanks to these joint admission sessions, so have we. "I understand completely. As I explained on the phone, these girls are excellent students, wonderful friends, and will make a fine addition to Nightshade. Unfortunately, one of my girls was a little too friendly at her last school, if you know what I mean."

My name is not mentioned, but the way Dr. Haskins barely looks at me, Headmistress Holly's gaze following, the implication is clear: at this school, it's my turn to play extra slutty.

I choke on a gasp.

"I've spoken with all three girls," she concludes, "and they assure me you will have no trouble from any of them. If you do, by all means, please alert me immediately and I'll rectify the situation posthaste."

"Outstanding," Headmistress Holly says, using another one of those headmistress words. "As you may or may not know, relations between Nightshade and the local townsfolk have recently become somewhat strained."

"Is that right?" Dr. Haskins says, fishing.

Headmistress Holly opens her mouth, looks at us girls, tightens her lips, then says, "You know how townsfolk are, certainly. They see this ornate architecture, the stained glass, the gargoyles. They hear our chapel bells every Sunday, and they can't

47

help but spread gossip about our students and their various activities during off hours. I assure you it's all unwarranted, and I mention it only so your girls can be aware that they must be on their best behavior and, of course, avoid being extra friendly."

She looks at me again, this time not so subtly.

"Of course." Dr. Haskins glances at her sleek Cartier watch resting on her elegant wrist.

The headmistress gets the hint and stands to signal the end of the meeting. "You do know that this late in the year, if one of your girls"—again with the eye roll in my direction—"were to get too friendly, as you so delicately put it, there would be no refund for the semester upon her dismissal."

"Of course," Dr. Haskins says, shaking Headmistress Holly's right hand. "Now, girls, I must run, but rest assured I leave you in capable hands here at Nightshade. Headmistress, thanks so much for your time in meeting us today. I assume you will help the girls get settled?"

"Of course," she says with a smile that doesn't quite meet her eyes. "And I assume you can show yourself out?"

We stand as Dr. Haskins exits, her heels clacking down the hallway.

When we turn from the door, Headmistress Holly stands just to our right, three room keys and a map in her outstretched hands. "Ladies," she says, her voice a tad more frosty than it was during her dealings with Dr. Haskins (not that we're exactly surprised), "I've circled your rooms on this map, and here are your keys. Your first task will be finding your own rooms and getting settled. Your second will be making it to dinner on time, promptly at six thirty. And your third will be showing up to your first classes tomorrow morning, no excuses. You'll find your schedules in your suite plus everything else you need. I hope you enjoy your . . . stay at Nightshade Conservatory for Exceptional Boys and Girls"—she looks squarely at me—"no matter how long or brief it might be.

"Good day, girls, and remember: here at Nightshade, you aren't merely fellow students; you're partners in learning.

"And never forget: if you need anything, my door is always open—from eleven till three Tuesdays and Thursdays, that is."

She smiles as we file past her.

I turn to wave our good-byes.

The heavy wooden door slams promptly in my face.

Alice and Cara are already steaming ahead, studying the map in Alice's hand.

This is definitely my last high school as a Sister. I don't care what it takes.

CHAPTER 5

"I don't understand why she threw me under the bus this time." I dump my single bag on the sterile claw-foot couch in the middle of our new dorm suite.

Cara and Alice are snickering as they check out the rooms, which look tiny and austere, perhaps because of all the dark wood flooring and creepy, gothic wainscoting along the entirety of the four-teen-foot ceilings.

Alice leans in her doorway, her long legs look-ing even longer in her skinny jeans. A big jeweled belt rests cockeyed on her model-narrow waist. "I, for one, am glad I won't be playing the role of super tramp this assignment."

I gape, about to say something snarky about how Alice couldn't look *less* like a tramp at the moment, but think better of it.

"Oh, give her time," Cara says to me from her own doorway. "Besides, Dr. Haskins did you a favor."

"A favor? By setting me up as a tramp? How so?"

"Think of it, girl. Now the Vamplayer will come looking for you, not the other way around."

I picture the tall boy in the alcove, his hand brushing away the redhead's curls, his confident stance, his cool eyes peering up at me as if he knew I'd been watching him all along. I shrug, unconvinced. "You know that's not how it usually works."

"Not usually," says Alice, "but at least she tried."

I sigh and retreat to my room to freshen up for dinner.

Mine is small but bright. Afternoon light filters through three gabled windows dominating most of each wall. A steel-framed bed is under the middle one, two bare wooden nightstands on either side, a matching dresser across from the foot of the bed.

Under another window is a simple desk, a rickety wooden chair shoved in as far as it will go. On the desk my schedule is wedged under the brass stand of an ancient lamp. I ignore it for now and look behind me to see if the other girls are watching.

The coast is clear.

As I do the first day of every assignment, I take my one-use, one-number pager and hide it beneath my nightstand. Crumpling up a clean sock and using it for cover, I shove both way in the back, where they're not readily visible from the front door or anywhere in the room but directly in front of it and then only while you're lying flat on the floor.

Next I change into simple black jeans and a gauzy black blouse over a silver tank top. I slip into charcoal shoes with enough heel to get me an inch higher but comfortable enough to walk the entire grounds of Nightshade before dinner if necessary.

When it's my turn in the communal bathroom, I freshen up with some lip gloss and a touch of Cara's perfume while my Sisters wait impatiently at the front door.

"So?" Alice says like a kid waiting to open presents Christmas morning. "Same drill as always? We'll split up and make the rounds, sit together at dinner, and see where we fit."

Cara and I look at each other. "I know where you'll fit best," she says to Alice as we walk out the door and into the hallway. "Right in some jock's arms."

"Or two," I say, "if he has a friend."

CHAPTER 6

I know I'm supposed to be doing recon right now and scouting the school for potential Vamplayers, but I skip the quad and the lawn and the gym and the track field, where kids normally congregate, and make a beeline for the cafeteria instead.

I know we still have a couple hours until dinner, but I'm a little famished from the long trip out— and not just for the red stuff.

It's a little known fact that most vampires are absolute sugar fiends. Like, crack addict–style sugar fiends. Some of us down sodas by the six-pack. Others literally rip open three or four sugar packets in a fast-food restaurant and glide into a blissful sugar coma as the granules dissolve on our greedy tongues.

They say this one girl at the Academy—I forget her name—went two full weeks, a record, without ingesting a single drop of blood by streamlining a case of Pixy Stix she'd ordered online.

My weakness, now and always, is candy. Chocolate preferably, bars of chocolate specifically, chocolate kisses in a pinch, chocolate squares if I'm desperate. But really, anything with straight-up sugar will do.

Yes, I know, we don't really digest our food so much as absorb it. And there's the rub: between feedings of blood consommé and braised blood clots and the occasional live vein during the holidays, there's nothing like a quick sugar high to rehydrate your cells and keep you humming along in Vamplayer-detecting mode.

This is what I hate about academies and conservatories and prep schools and the like: assigned meal times.

Public schools are much better when it comes to enabling sugar addicts to get their fix. I mean, between the vending machines, candy bar fund-raisers, the parking lots smack-dab in the middle of two convenience stores and three gas stations, a Sister never wants for sugar when she's assigned to a public school.

But academies, especially conservatories, are so rigid. No quick sugar fixes unless you cozy up to the kitchen staff and persuade them to break you off a nibble of baking chocolate or, if necessary, a marshmallow or a macaroon.

I hear clanging dishes down a distant hall and know I'm finally heading in the right direction. *Bring the map next time, Lily!*

I peel off toward the sound, walking what feel like miles and miles of empty, twenty-foot-high hallways lined on one side with vast stained glass windows and on the other with stone.

I pass a few kids, mostly girls with long thin legs and swinging short skirts. I give them a casual nod, get none in return, and fantasize about sinking my fangs into their stupid chichi throats to teach them a lesson about common civility. *Down, girl, down.*

The clinking grows louder and louder, and I enter through two giant doors that lead to a sprawling, if empty, cafeteria.

It seems to stretch, like the rest of the school, for miles. It's as if the Jolly Green Giant designed it for himself but had to sell it at a loss during the recession.

I count at least three dozen tables with at least a dozen chairs at each. They are clean and smell of bleach, and some still even look damp.

My flats are soft and silent on the tiled cafeteria floor as I pass through the sea of empty tables and shoved-in chairs.

I hear hissing steam, laughter, clinking plates, and rattling silverware and know I'm in the right place. I can almost taste the bittersweet chocolate or maybe even a squirt of chocolate syrup or perhaps just the last of the maraschino cherry juice at the bottom of a jar.

I'm so eager my fangs quiver, and I nearly barge straight into the kitchen proper.

Then I hear this and pause: "There's no way Luke Skywalker could beat Captain Kirk in a fair fight."

Oh boy, this ought to be good.

I stand just outside the red swinging double doors, complete with grimy portholes at the top center like you see on cruise ships, and listen in.

A hearty baritone voice says, "Define fair fight, Zander."

"What always constitutes a fair fight, Grover?" the other asks, his voice clipped and masculine, less melodic. "Identical weapons, identical uniforms."

Water hisses out of what sounds like a nozzle gun.

I try to put faces with sounds, but the voices

seem so close to the doors that I can't risk looking through the windows.

"You're telling me a standard Starship Enterprise uniform is going to give Kirk some untold advantage over a Jedi Knight?"

"Grover, have you ever actually examined a Jedi Knight's uniform up close and personal?"

"As personal as you can get at a Mega-Con light-saber signing, my dear boy."

"Then you know it's much baggier, much fruitier than Kirk's uniform, which is much more stream-lined and—"

"Define fruitier."

I can't stand it anymore. I shove through the doors like an outlaw in some old western and stand, hands on my hips. "Yeah, define—"

But I never get to finish my sentence. A stream of hot water splashes my face.

And my hair.

My neck.

My shoulders.

And my midsection.

"Oh. My. God." I hear the Grover person (I think) screaming. "Zander, put it down. Put the hose down!"

Zander (I think) gasps, and the dishwashing spray gun he's been holding hits the floor, squirming like a snake that's just been grabbed by the tail and saturating us with fine, hot jets of water.

Suddenly chocolate (baking, syrup, or otherwise) is the last thing on my mind.

CHAPTER 7

"You see, miss, uh, I mean, ma'am, it's just that, well, we're not used to actual women being in the cafeteria," the one who shall be known as Grover stammers as he hands me yet another thin white cotton towel from the wrought iron bar on his dorm suite bathroom wall.

"What?" I keep drying my hair. "You're telling me it's an all-male kitchen staff."

They bite their lips, snickering in the doorway.

"What my roommate means, miss," says the one who shall be known as Zander, "is that we're not used to having *girls* in the kitchen. Like, you know, actual student girls."

"Like actual hot student girls."

I glare, then look at my supposed-to-knock-'em-dead-on-the-first-night black blouse covering my sopping wet silver tank top and see pieces of white towel lint sticking all over it. "Well, what were you two doing in there anyway? Having a quick water fight before dinner?"

With my head out from under a towel for the first time since they dragged me from the cafeteria to their suite, I notice the boys' soggy, dirty aprons.

"We work there," Grover says proudly or maybe defensively; it's hard to tell when your ears are full of water. "Nightshade gives us a third off our tuition every semester if we handle kitchen duty before and after classes. So, again, we're really sorry."

I instantly feel cruddy.

Like these poor guys don't have it bad enough slaving away in the kitchen twice a day on top of regular school. And God knows how the Nightshade snobs must torture them over it.

I give up on drying myself, wrap the towel around my shoulders like some dazed prizefighter, and sit on the closed toilet lid. "No, it's my fault. I shouldn't have barged in on you like that."

Grover, big as a house, nudges Zander. "She does have a point, dude."

Zander is nearly four inches taller than Grover and a third his weight. He's not skinny, per se. He's just lean, although his roguishly handsome face is just fleshy enough to dimple when he smiles, crookedly, which he does amazingly often.

"Yeah," he says, leaning casually on the doorjamb. "What were you barging in for anyway?"

"Well"—I sigh dramatically—"I was just looking for a snack before dinner. You know, something sweet like a Laffy Taffy or Hershey's Kiss, when I heard the most asinine argument ever and—"

"Oh, please, please, please tell me you didn't hear that," Zander squeaks, face growing three shades of red and two of purple. He puts his long fingers together in a supplicating gesture. "Please, oh please, say you didn't hear us arguing about—"

"Skywalker versus Kirk," I say gleefully. "Sure did. Every word of it. It was very . . . illuminating."

Grover walks away, probably out of embarrassment, and disappears around the corner.

"I can't wait to share your findings at the first possible opportunity over dinner tonight. Is there a microphone available in the cafeteria or perhaps a blow horn? A podium and slide-show screen? Because I really think everyone deserves to hear it verbatim. Hey, here's an idea. Maybe you two can reenact it. Wouldn't that be cool?"

Zander hangs his head. His dirty blond curls dangle near his bushy brunet eyebrows. In the irresistible department, it's like peanut butter meeting chocolate—and not just 'cause I'm starved for sugar. When he raises his head, I admire his hazel eyes, his adorable pug nose, and his smile.

He looks me in the eye and says, "Well, hold up. If that's why you barged in, then whose side were you going to take? Obviously you came in loaded for bear, so fess up. Who would win that one?"

I snort. This one's quick. "Kirk, of course. His uniform quails on Skywalker's."

"Thank you." He moves in for a quick high five, which of course I deny.

He mumbles, "Oh right," and leans against the wall.

When Grover returns, he has a handful of both Laffy Taffies *and* Hershey's Kisses. I should probably be surprised he happens to have both of my favorite types of candy, but from the looks of him, this kid has every type of candy in his possession.

"For you, m'lady," he says, handing them over with a mock Renaissance bow and a trilling motion of one massive, pink hand.

"You, good sir, are almost forgiven," I say around a mouthful of divine melting chocolate, shoving the Laffy Taffies in my pocket for later. And, no, I won't be sharing them with Alice or Cara. "I shouldn't be taking candy from a stranger," I say to Grover coyly, the instant sugar rush turning me vaguely coquettish, "so let's introduce ourselves and then I won't feel so guilty."

"I'm Grover, and this beanpole here is Zander. And you are?"

"Lily. I'm—"

"New," Zander finishes for me. "Yeah, we'd re-member seeing someone like you around."

I can't tell if it's a compliment or another jab, but at this point I'll take what I can get.

Zander nudges Grover and shows him his watch. Both stand at attention.

"Something wrong?" I look down at my damp chest to make sure I'm not having some kind of wardrobe malfunction or something.

"No," Zander says, "it's just, dinner is in an hour, and if we don't finish cleaning first we'll get docked and have to start even earlier tomorrow, so . . ."

I stand, the heavy toilet seat making clatter-ing noises to further my already significant level of absolute embarrassment. "Go, go," I say forcefully, shooing them like a mom sending her kids outside for some much needed exercise. "Far be it from me to get you in any more trouble."

Zander smiles, heading for the door.

Grover says, "Can you show yourself out?"

"I'd love to. That will give me some time to lay some booby traps around here. I'm thinking water balloons above the doors, slime in your soda cans, and of course fake snakes in your peanut brittle jars. You know what they say about payback, right, boys?"

They grin and cut out of the room, talking, laughing, shambling all over each other on their way.

I stand and am not surprised when I notice the Boba Fett toilet seat I've been sitting on or the Wookie shower curtain or the matching Darth Vader electric toothbrushes. I'm not even shocked by the green Yoda throw pillows on both perfectly made beds.

"Well," I mutter as I walk out of the suite, "you have to admire their consistency, if not their taste."

CHAPTER 8

"**S**peaking of taste," a deep, rich voice says from the inky halls, "first impressions are so important, aren't they, dear?"

"Indeed," an equally rich, though decidedly feminine voice, says. "I guess it's true what they say: the new girl *is* a tramp."

I turn, gasping, ready to unload my considerable immortal fury on my fellow students. Instead I see the two shadowy figures I saw speaking outside Headmistress Holly's window during our brief orientation earlier this afternoon.

"W-w-what did you just say?" I manage to stammer, though it's hard when half your face is under a towel and what's visible is covered in runny mascara and smudged lipstick.

"Nothing, dear." The guy is taller in person, crisper, leaner, cuter—if that's possible—than he looked from Headmistress Holly's window. "Just that, well, you couldn't wait until your second day to seduce a couple of work release geeks? From the cafeteria, no less?"

"Too right." The stunning girl's eyes are magnetically green and intoxicating. "At least pretend to be hard to get for a day or two before giving the milk away for free. Any tramp worth her salt knows that much."

Zander and Grover's door is still open, though they are long gone, giving us a clear shot of their Star Wars poster–covered wall, to say nothing of their prolific action figure collection displayed on several perfectly straight shelves and, of course, the scale model spacecraft hanging on fishing wire from every available inch of ceiling space.

I stow the towel behind my back and ignore the wet tendrils still covering the other half of my face. "Whatever do you mean?"

"It's all a matter of taste, Lily." The redhead looks me up and down the way a garbage man sizes up a stained mattress in the gutter. "It's one thing to be promiscuous." She hangs on to the guy's sleeve. "But at least try to be a little discriminating, huh?"

"What? When? How do you know my name?"

She sizes me up. "You're at Nightshade, where everybody knows everybody else—and everything *about* everybody else. You're Lily, the easy one. Then there's Cara, I believe, the . . . multicultural one. I hear Alice is the smart one."

I snort. The smart one? Obviously they don't know everything here at Nightshade.

"Hmm." I tousle my hair to try to at least look presentable. "Then I'm at a disadvantage because I have no idea who you two are."

She takes it as it was intended: a massive slight. Her face is not quite as red as her flowing, gorgeous tresses but close enough to make me smile.

"Bianca Ridley. Of the Manhattan Ridleys."

Yeah, like that means anything to a vampire who spends half her time shut away in an academy for the undead and the rest in boring high schools deep in the Midwest.

"Tristan." The hunk, er, guy extends a long, pale hand. "Tristan Winters."

I smirk. Hmm, a Vamplayer name if ever I've

heard one. I take his hand, which is dry and papery, another sure sign.

His eyes are a deep brown, leaning toward the dark chocolate side. His long hair is thick and a deep shade of black: so black the shiny locks almost glisten in the soft light of the stone-walled halls.

"Well, it's nice to meet you both. Not that I need to defend myself, but whatever you think happened in there didn't. The boys were only helping me dry off."

"Sure, it didn't." Bianca loops her arm in Tristan's and tugs near as if a chill has wafted through the hall.

If it has, I can't feel it. Maybe she's just cold from the inside out.

Tristan's chin fits perfectly atop her head.

Feeling like a voyeur watching them nuzzle, I clear my throat and walk past them. "Anyway," I say as my arm brushes Tristan's, "it was nice meeting you. I'm sure I'll be seeing you around."

"Oh, you will," Bianca says. "Maybe next time you'll be a little more presentable."

I stride away, mumbling loud enough for her to hear, "Maybe next time you'll be a little more hospitable."

I can't tell if the chuckling is from Bianca or Tristan.

CHAPTER 9

"Time to go to Plan B," I say at dinner, which basically consists of Alice, Cara, and me shoving food around our plates and twisting bits of mashed potatoes and peas into our napkins so it looks to the other students like we ate something.

"What?" Cara says, smiling. Her gorgeous face lights up. "What happened to Plan A?"

"Yeah." Alice barely looks at us and gives a brisk princess wave to a nearby table of burly, thick-necked jocks. "We usually don't go to Plan B until at least our second day. What happened?"

I nod at Tristan and Bianca, who hold court at a table full of the rich and beautiful. "They saw me coming out of their room"—I nod at Zander and Grover, who hustle with heavy bus pans—"see-through and soaked from head to toe."

"What?" both girls say loudly.

Zander breaks into a grin and speeds into the kitchen.

"How?" Cara says.

"More importantly, why?" Alice says.

"It's a long story." After telling them, though, I realize it's actually pretty short. And not entirely flattering.

"We're supposed to be doing recon," Alice says in her First Sister voice, "not stuffing our sweet teeth with the Official Star Wars Lightsaber Duel Reenactment Club."

Second Sister Cara is a little less blunt but no less judgmental. "That's not like you."

"It was an accident, you guys. I was supposed to quick pop in, pop out, but Zander's hose went off and Grover lost it and I got all wet and—"

"Hold up, hold up," Alice interrupts through a burst of contagious giggles, reminding me why I like her despite the fact that she can be a Grade A, First Sister snob. "Are we still in the kitchen by this point, or are you describing what happened in the geeks' room?"

Ignoring the insinuation, I say, "They're not geeks exactly. They're just not your type."

"Oh, you mean they're not handsome, athletic, popular, or fun? Okay, well, now I know what you saw in them."

Cara pretends to sip the apple juice from her full glass, in case anyone's looking. The football thick necks are. "We certainly can't pass her off as the school tramp now. She's lost all her street cred."

"Well, if you guys insist . . ." Alice's voice trails off.

The guys she's been flirting with all dinner long stand and shuffle out, giving her backward glances as they go.

"I guess I'll do what I do so well." She mock sighs, quickly standing.

"What, you mean taste-testing your way through the student body to find the Vamplayer?" I say.

"It's a dirty job, girls, but somebody has to do it. Might as well be somebody good at it." She walks away, leaving her tray behind.

I gasp. "Was that a dig, Cara?"

"Yeah, for sure it was, Lily."

We share a laugh, but Cara seems distracted.

As I sort our dishes and stack our trays, I look up to see why.

"Hey, Cara." A group of girls have miraculously appeared at our table. They're not wearing uniforms, but I can tell they're cheerleaders by the way they walk in formation and blink in unison. Takes one to know one, after all. "We were hoping you'd sit with us tonight."

Cara beams. "Oh, that would have been nice. Listen, what are you guys doing now?"

A petite girl with a great body says, "Going to practice our cheers, of course."

"Well, can I join you?"

Without an answer, they escort her away with perfectly manicured hands and delighted squeals.

She manages to wave at me behind her back.

Plan B is definitely in effect. The one where Alice does her trampy, baddy-baddy thing, Cara does her sporty, goodie-goodie thing, and I do my thing, whatever *that* is.

Either way, by hook or by crook, we are supposed to infiltrate Nightshade, sniff out the Vamplayer, and bring him down before he can do any harm. At least that's Plan B in theory.

I watch Zander scuttle around under endless loads of bus trays.

It doesn't seem to be working out too hot so far.

CHAPTER 10

The track is a nice one, made out of the soft, bumpy material that's great on your feet and even better on your joints. It's five in the morning and still dark as I finish my fifth lap. My legs and shoulders are finally loosening up after a tense first day and night at Nightshade.

Alice and Cara are still asleep. Well, I know Cara's still asleep. I heard her snoring softly when I crept out of the dorm room fifteen minutes ago, pass key in one hand, black running shoes in the other. Alice? Well, Alice never came home last night. Not that I'm worried. That's part of Plan B, if not her charm.

I've never been quite sure why guys flock to Alice

like hungry vampires to a slaughterhouse. Sure, she's pretty, but Cara certainly is too and I've never really considered myself chopped liver.

No, it's something more than her long legs, flat stomach, blue eyes, and blonde hair. It's more than her provocative grin, her flirty ways, her gum popping, and the way she twists a strand of hair around her finger all day long.

Some girls are just like that. Guys seem to know they'll enjoy their company, and Alice genuinely does. I mean, we joke that she's never met a jock she didn't like, but it's really true. They can be dumb as dirt, mean as snakes, dull as dishwater, or high as a kite, and Alice will find a way to enjoy their company.

She's been on dates to ice cream parlors, rock concerts, museums, state fairs, foreign films, drive-throughs. One guy even took her cow tipping; I kid you not. She always returns (the next morning, of course) raving about how wonderful and intoxicating and refreshing it was.

I wish it were that simple for me. I wish I could ignore the fact that I'm never going to die and the guys are and just have fun with the mortals while I'm here. It sure would make high school more fun if I could let myself go and actually date some of these hotties I'm here to protect, but I can't seem to unplug those thoughts of the future.

Alice? There is nothing but today for Alice. This moment, this school, this guy or that guy or that one over there. That's as far as she thinks.

I envy her attitude, and I pity her too.

Who knows where she is at five on a Tuesday morning? Lying on some guy's bed or couch or floor. Waking in a strange room, wondering where she is, taking that long, sad walk of shame to our dorm.

No, thanks. Not for me. I'd rather roll out of my own bed, thank you very much, hit the alarm before it disturbs Cara, and be out here on my own, free of all my dread and responsibilities.

So, yeah, it's just me out here in the dark, but frankly that's the way I like it. Being a Sister is awesome, and I wouldn't trade it for the world, but even a Sister gets tired of her own Sisters, you know?

Dawn's bluish-orange stillness approaches. All is blissfully, Sister-free quiet.

Until . . . until I hear strong breathing behind me, the scent of a young, hungry male (aren't they all?) heavy on the crisp morning air.

I don't turn, because I've already done enough lame things in my first twenty-four hours here. I just slow my pace to near human levels and glide—make that coast—through another half lap before the steady breathing draws ever closer.

Rounding the curve onto my sixth lap, I'm looser than ever, skin glowing, if not exactly sweating, when a large presence looms to my left, on the inside edge of the track.

"Imagine meeting you here, Lily," a deep, languid voice says.

"Likewise, Tristan." I run a little faster just to liven things up a tad. As I suspected, he keeps perfect pace with me, not even slowing when he slicks his hair behind each ear.

When I see no one tailing us, I ask, "Where's your better half this morning?"

He doesn't answer but picks up speed, nudging past me.

I watch the back of his snug track pants and pick up the pace.

"Getting her beauty sleep, of course."

"Of course."

He remains steady at my side. "Not that we're exclusive," he says casually, as if he's mentioning the weather.

"Really?" I say, purposely sounding surprised. "She sure seems to think so."

"Bianca?" he says idly, finally glancing over with those deep, dark chocolate eyes. He smirks. "You must not know her very well then."

"True, but she sure looked possessive in the hall yesterday."

He shrugs his broad shoulders. "Let's just say Bianca is all about appearances." We run a while longer before he says, "No doubt she clung protectively to many of her suitors throughout the day."

"Reeeeally? And how many suitors does she have?"

He grins. "Like I said, you don't know her very well."

Half a lap later, I ask, "Well, how well do *you* know her?" I try to say it like I'm only mildly inquisitive rather than downright curious—which I am only in a professional capacity, of course.

"My, my." He nudges me. "It is a bit early to get so personal, don't you think?"

I shake my head. "What I mean to say is, how long have you known Bianca?"

"Ah, that is more like it. Well, I would like to think we have known each other forever, but I transferred here only earlier this semester, so . . ."

He says more, but I don't hear it. The deep, dark eyes, the pale complexion, the superhuman speed, the stilted, almost foreign accent and he *just transferred here*? I try not to get too excited. Rarely do I spot the Vamplayer on the second day. And, truth be told, one of the other Sisters usually spots him first.

Contrary to popular belief, vampires can't see one another until we choose to reveal ourselves. Mortals seem to think we can see right through each other's skin to the nonbeating heart, the flaccid lungs, the fangs wedged high in our gum lines, but in fact it's quite difficult to spot a vampire even when you know what to look for.

Unfortunately, the only sure way to get a Vamplayer to show his true colors is to expose them yourself. So unless I want to blow my cover first, and way too soon, it's really a guessing game until Alice, Cara, and I weigh all the evidence and risk outing ourselves to reveal his true identity.

Like I said, we're not quite there yet.

I glide over to the right, not because I'm scared of him exactly but to get a better look.

He doesn't glance over but continues loping down the track.

I subconsciously pick up the pace in gradual increments.

His black jacket with two broad white stripes on each arm is open to his waist, revealing a white V-neck

T-shirt that hugs the curves of his manly chest the same way he hugs the inside corner as we round the far end of the track. His shoes are top of the line and match his track suit, as if he ordered the set online or perhaps got them for free while modeling for *GQ*.

For another two laps, he matches me stride for stride, his firm body making light work of mile two.

I'm not even close to capacity (yes, vampires are incredibly fast), but I'm keeping it on the down low in case (a) any mere mortals are watching and (b) Tristan isn't the Vamplayer, however unlikely that seems.

He says little more as we run, apparently growing more winded with each lap. I smile. If he's acting, he's not half bad. I mean, I genuinely believe he's tired.

Finally he slows down, then stops a lap later, his hands on his knees, his breathing labored.

I stop too because, let's face it: it's just plain rude to keep running when your partner's about to pass out on you.

He's so good, pretending to be exhausted. He's even sweating, a rare skill among Vamplayers, though not entirely unheard of, I suppose. Not that, as Third Sister, I know everything there is to know about Vamplayers, but here are the basics.

Vamplayers aren't a particular breed of vampire,

necessarily, just a very special type. Just as in the mortal world, we all have our roles in the vampiric world. There are the Scavengers, loner vamps who walk the earth feasting on beast and man alike. There are the Saviors and the Sisters, the hunters and the protectors. There are the Ancients, the rule makers who oversee our communities and enforce our laws.

There are Royal vampires, those vamps who were born of two vampire parents, not made like the rest of us. There is even a superior race of Original vampires; the first of our kind, nearly godlike creatures rarely seen. Very few of the Originals remain. Instead, their bloodline lives on in the cells and DNA of the Royals.

And then there are the Vamplayers: normal vampires who just happen to enjoy wreaking havoc on the mortal world by turning typical, suburban, innocent high schools into hotbeds of brand-new vampires, fresh for the feasting.

Like all guys, some Vamplayers are strong; some are weak. All are drop-dead gorgeous and have an insatiable bloodlust for young nubile flesh. A few have even been Royals, though Cara, Alice, and I have never had the displeasure of battling one so strong as a born vampire. Most are just like us, regular old vampires only nastier, greedier, and far sneakier. Like this one, maybe, with his sweaty brow and trying to act like he can't outsprint some poor, mortal girl six laps to her one.

"You all right?" I say with a slightly superior tone, standing tall, hands on hips, barely breathing, though Tristan doesn't need to know why.

"Sure," he says, voice strong—at least between gasps. "Fine, great!"

I laugh, grabbing a towel from along the chain link fence bordering the track. I toss it his way.

"Thanks. I'm good." He throws it back, a little harder.

I shrug and pretend to dry off, though my skin is already quite parched since—that's right—vampires don't sweat.

He stands, pressing his hands at the small of his back and leaning over at the waist, side to side, until he catches his breath. "Well," he says, shaking his legs out, "that was the best workout I've had since I've gotten here. Do you run every morning?"

I hide my delight. The Vamplayer has asked *me* to work out with him every morning? This is too rich. Wait'll the other Sisters hear. They always think it's such a waste of time to exercise every morning, but this time it's finally paid off.

"Not every morning," I hedge.

He winks. "Well, I look forward to running with you *most* mornings then, Lily."

We walk off the track, following the sidewalk into the back entrance of the school.

Tristan opens the door for me, bowing slightly and making a courtly gesture. "Ladies first."

I plunge ahead to tell the other Sisters as Tristan makes a quick exit down the opposite hallway.

I feel a vague presence at my side and turn quickly to see who it might be. Almost running into a tall, lanky figure, I gasp. "Zander?"

He barely sees me, watching instead as Tristan, looking every bit the Olympic type, jaunts toward the boys' locker room.

"Lily?" Zander says, his apron over his shoulder, his eyes sleepy and, dare I say, disappointed?

CHAPTER
11

The first class I have with Tristan and Bianca is fifth period PE. Fortunately, Alice and Cara are in it as well. Unfortunately, Alice is acting like she barely knows us.

I'm still feeling limber from my run with Tristan, although I'm a little miffed at the way Zander blew me off during lunch when he and Grover shared a table for two. It looked like Grover was going to wave me over and ask me to join them, something I would have enjoyed after four straight hours of mind-numbing morning classes. (You can hear the Emancipation Proclamation only so many times before it loses its poetry, you know?)

But with a quick jab from Zander, Grover stared down at his tray, unblinking.

I huffed from the cafeteria a few minutes later, tossed my uneaten yogurt and fruit cup into the nearest trash can (sorry, starving kids in third world countries), and spent the period watching Cara practice cheers with her new BFFs out on the quad.

We're in the locker room now, Cara and I slipping into our red shorts and black tank tops, Nightshade's school colors.

A few minutes before class is supposed to start, Alice stumbles in and hustles over but only because her locker is right next to ours.

"Where have you been?" I whisper. "You never came in last night."

Cara looks even more upset. "This is the first time I've seen you all day, Alice!"

"Relax." Alice grabs her stuff and quickly slams her locker shut. "It's called blending in, okay? Deal."

"Blend in, fine," Cara says as Alice drifts away, "but tell a Sister where you are, 'kay?"

"'Kay," Alice mimics, rushing to Bianca and her crew, turning her back on us as soon and as often as she can.

Bianca looks at her, and Cara and I hold our

nonexistent breath in case Alice is assuming too much too soon. But Bianca opens her arms and gives the First Sister a big, fat first order hug.

Cara and I share a *Do you believe that?* look before leaning to tie our shoes, attempting not to look quite so jealous.

"That was sooooo fun last night," Bianca gushes.

Alice quickly slips into her PE uniform. "Wasn't it?"

"That was pretty sweet!" Alice says as a few more of Bianca's identically pretty friends gather around her. "I never knew skinny-dipping could be so fun."

"Mmmmmm. It's much more fun when you invite the boys along."

Cara and I look at each other and mouth the words, *Skinny-dipping?* and *Invite the boys along?* We're far from prudes, but this is too much.

We slam our lockers and bound out to the gym floor, where a short, paunchy man in too-snug coaching shorts and a too-baggy golf shirt holds a clipboard.

"Names?" he says.

"Lily Fielding." I spot Zander and Grover lurking on the sidelines, Grover practically spilling out of and over his ginormous gym shorts while Zander basically floats in his.

"Cara Sierra," she says proudly.

Grover drags Zander to us. "Hello, Lily." Grover extends a warm, meaty hand. "And who is this delectable creature you've brought with you to class today?"

Never one to discriminate, she extends her long fingers and says, "Cara, and you are?"

"This is Grover," I say, since the man himself seems to be particularly tongue-tied at the moment, "and this fellow with the scowly expression and mismatched tube socks is Zander. I met them yesterday."

Zander shakes Cara's hand brusquely, looks to see if I'm right about his socks, and groans.

A burst of laughter comes from the girls' locker room as the door opens and Bianca, Alice, and several beautiful drones stream out, looking as if they've just heard Dane Cook's new album at a private prerelease party or something.

Tristan stands aloof among a group of bigger, dopier guys.

Like magnets, Bianca and Alice steer toward them.

Alice fits in perfectly.

I nudge Cara, but she's already scoping the scene.

"I've got to admit," she says, "that girl's good."

I nod begrudgingly. "Well, she's not First Sister for nothing."

Cara snorts and nudges me. "Nah, she ain't *that* good. She's only First Sister because she's been here the longest. You and me, we'll get our day." She smiles.

I smile back.

But what I'm really thinking is, *Yeah, but when?*

The guy with the clipboard and *Coach Wannamaker* monogrammed on his red polyester shirt blows his whistle, and we all stand at attention (funny how some things never change). From a plastic cart at his side, he drags out a mesh bag full of multicolored balls.

Half the class (the pretty, chosen, Bianca clones) cheer.

The other half (everybody else) groan.

"That's right. It's the second Tuesday of the month, children, and that means . . ." He waits for us to respond.

I follow Grover and Zander's lead as they say listlessly, "Dodgeball derby."

Simultaneously, Tristan, Bianca and her crew, and of course Alice cheer, "Dodgeball *derby*!"

I nudge Zander, leaning close to his warm, pink ear. "How come they're all so happy and we're so sad?"

He smirks. "You'll see."

Coach Wannamaker reaches into the bag and tosses a ball at a random student.

"You know the drill," he grumps, tossing balls willy-nilly with his hairy, beefy arms. "If you get a red ball, report to the visitors' side of the gym. If you get a black ball, report to the home side."

Turns out I was wrong. He's not tossing out the balls randomly at all.

A pattern emerges. The red balls land on our side of the gym, first to Grover, then Zander, then me, then Cara, and then to an odd assortment of freaks, geeks, misfits, and losers.

Meanwhile the black balls zip over to Tristan, Bianca, Alice, and the like.

By the time all the balls have been tossed, the home side of the court looks like a photo shoot for an Abercrombie & Fitch catalog while the poor visitors' side looks like two short busses pulled up and dumped us off after a somber visit to the local cemetery.

"This sucks major." Grover stomps once like a disgruntled third grader whose brother dumped his ice cream cone in the sandbox.

"What'd we do wrong?" I say.

RUSTY FISCHER

"You?" He looks Cara and me up and down but not in a salacious way. "You two belong over there."

"Yeah," Zander says, "you two made the mistake of talking to us while Coach Wannamaker was handing out the dodge balls. Guilt by association, I'm afraid."

"What's wrong with these balls?" Cara squeezes hers like an overripe cantaloupe.

"Oh, nothing a few dozen pounds of air pressure wouldn't cure." Grover places his under one armpit and makes gaseous noises to the delight of our reject team and the obvious disgust of Bianca and her glamorous pals.

I squeeze mine, and he's right. It's like half the air has been let out. On purpose. The nerve!

I peer toward the home team side and watch Alice bouncing her big, fat, black ball on the basketball court like she's preparing for liftoff or perhaps a tryout with the Harlem Globetrotters. "Well, that's not fair at all."

"Welcome to Nightshade," Zander says.

"Welcome to high school." Grover sighs.

Without warning, Coach Wannamaker blows his whistle twice. Suddenly the two dozen perfectly inflated balls launch. It's like a scene out of one of

90

those Japanese movies where an army of archers shoot so many arrows into the sky that they blot out the sun. You can almost hear the whoosh as the balls fill the air, advancing steadily toward our pitiful team.

Instinctively, Cara and I shove Zander and Grover behind us and catch two balls expertly, as if we've been trained to do this. Come to think of it, considering how many times we play this game every year, the Academy should absolutely have a Dodgeball Tactics for the PE Averse class.

On the opposite side of the court, two beautiful people slump to the side.

Cara and I look at each other, smile, and launch the balls back to the home side, nailing two pretty girls, who scream, rub their shoulders, and limp to the sidelines.

Zander and Grover guffaw and hand us their dodge balls.

"Sweet!" Grover says.

"Wicked!" Zander says. "It's like Slam the Super-models Day."

Double-handed now, Cara and I take out four more hottie hopefuls, the half-inflated balls making thwap-sting-slap sounds as they land on human flesh, leaving big, fat red welts where once there was only flawless skin.

One girl falls so hard, her perfect derriere squeaks for several feet across the gym floor.

The other girl gets knocked back into the blue gym mats strapped to the wall behind the basket, where she lands in a heap on the floor. Whap.

"You're outta the game," Coach Wannamaker shouts.

Thwack-slap.

"Out."

Whap.

Whap!

Whap!

"Out. All three of you, gone!"

I peek at Zander's face. His mouth is wide open, his eyes nearly as big.

Meanwhile, Grover is simply drooling.

I sneer. I know it looks to humans as if we vampires are moving quickly and have catlike reflexes, but the fact is that the world moves slowly. Our metabolisms are so fast that it's like our senses are always on red alert. *Running to stand still* is what I call it.

So when a ball comes flying at us, it's not that we move so fast; it's that the ball goes so slowly we have extra time to avoid it. To mortals the world is going in fast-forward, but to us it feels like the pause button is always on.

"Oh, this is awesome!" Grover pats his gym shorts. "Where is my cell phone video camera when I need it?"

Eventually only Bianca, Tristan, and Alice are left standing after our full frontal assault. Cara and I march steadily toward the half-court line, picking up ripe black dodge balls along the way and launching them with expert precision.

Bianca evades them surprisingly well for a mere mortal, but then half the time she's either hiding behind Tristan or Alice, alternately shrieking and protecting her precious hair.

Alice fights hard, though. Ball after ball zips by my head, and I want to shout, "We're Sisters, remember?"

Her eyes have an almost religious zeal when she targets us again and again.

"Who gave this witch a vendetta?" Cara says as a ball narrowly misses her left ear and nails Grover in the belly.

"Ummphfuzzlesnot," he mumbles, falling to the floor and rolling on his side in exquisite agony.

Like any good soldier, Zander sacrifices himself to

drag his friend safely off the court, but Bianca and Alice show no mercy, peppering him with dodge balls the entire way. They land with deadly accuracy, thwacking against his pale skin and leaving instant bruises.

To silence them, I take careful aim and nail Bianca in the arm.

"Hey!" She steps forward as if she's going to launch a ball-free attack with her fists.

Forgetting myself, I walk to greet her.

"Now, now, dear," Tristan says calmly with that snooty voice of his, expertly dodging the balls Cara and I throw. "Where are your manners? No one likes a sore loser."

"Too right," Bianca says, rubbing her arm and staring daggers at me. "Where would I be without you, my love?" She curtsies and exits the game to the cheers of her adoring fans, er, friends.

Alice, Tristan, Cara, and I square off, mere feet from each other, dodge balls flying rapidly from one to the other in an endless dizzying cycle. It's like our arms don't even pause, zipping and zapping and finding balls and flinging them like human—well, almost human—tennis ball machines.

With every near miss on our side, their side roars—and vice versa.

Balls are whizzing so fast, our sneakers squeaking so loudly on the gym floor, it's like a cacophony of jungle noises in the middle of the gym.

At one point Tristan trips, their side gasps, and Cara uses the opportunity to launch an aerial assault straight at his face. (Hey, all's fair in love and dodgeball, pretty boy.)

Alice manages to deflect one projectile just in time but has to dive for the second ball to do so.

I see the gap, heave two more right away, and take Tristan out with a sound pounding on each shoulder.

Whack-slam!

Thwack-slap!

He falls, laughing.

Several beautiful girls, Alice included, rush to help him off the court.

"Dang," Cara says, "this dude's good."

"I know, right?"

"You think," she says, eyebrows arching, "he could be our man?"

"You tell me."

We watch him limp off, either acting like he thinks a human would to throw us off the scent or actually feeling pain.

"Well," she grumbles, picking up a few balls for

our last assault, "he's either really good or really bad, you know?"

"I do." I juggle a few balls to stay loose.

Alice takes to the court, standing defiantly, but the wind has left her sails.

Despite the cheers from the beautiful people's side, she lobs two easy balls at us. When we catch them, Alice waves in defeat, turning her back to us without a word and retreating to her side.

Cara and I exchange questioning glances, but too soon we are deluged by our team. They're hugging us, cheering, Grover and Zander at the head of the pack.

Zander hugs me amidst the furor, and it's so warm, so soft, so good I never want to let him go.

"Ahem." Grover squeezes in closer. "Group hug!"

Is that disappointment I see in Zander's eyes? Or relief?

CHAPTER 12

"What is up with that girl?" Cara says later as we lounge in our dorm suite, nursing our dodge-ball wounds and getting group dissed by one Sister. Cara's done for the night but looks ready to party in her tight red jeans and sporty white pullover.

"I dunno," I say around a straw full of fresh O negative from the care package we found on our doorstep, return addressed Afterlife Academy and containing a short good-luck note from Dr. Haskins. "I've seen her go undercover before, but this is deep undercover. Even for her."

Cara shakes her head, reaching for a second bag of A positive. She drinks it carefully, almost daintily, to avoid spilling any of the red stuff on her jersey-style white top. "If we're right, if Tristan is the Vamplayer and Bianca is his most obvious target, then I can understand Alice's enthusiasm for infiltrating the beautiful people here at Nightshade. But it's the Sisterhood of Dangerous Girlfriends, plural, not the Dangerous Girlfriend, singular. Am I right?"

I nod. She's so fired up, I'm tempted to give her a fist bump across the coffee table. "Maybe she's so eager to stay First Sister, she's just trying to show us both up."

"Wouldn't be the first time. Remember that school last year in Kentucky, or was it Nebraska, where she thought she had the Vamplayer identified in our first week, only she didn't tell us and ended up calling the Saviors on some poor goth punk wannabe?"

"Was he the guy who peed his pants when they busted through the boys' locker room ceiling?"

"No, girl, that was in Florida last year. Where you been?"

I shrug. "Or how about that time she thought she saw fangs on a guy, called the Saviors, and they came crashing in on a dramatic reading of *Laurel and Hardy Meet Dracula*?"

She snickers, finishes her last bag of blood, and

sighs. Her long legs stretch over the armrest and dangle, crossed at the ankles. She fidgets slowly, steadily, stirring dust bunnies on the dark, rich, almost ancient hardwood floor beneath her feet.

It's dusk, the day mostly done, but soft white light from the wrought iron sconces sift shadows through the common area.

Cara stands and walks two bags of blood toward Alice's empty, still-made bed to place there like the vampire equivalent of mints on her pillow.

There is a soft knock at our door, two quick raps. Alice herself swoops in, a manic and almost unwelcome ball of energy in our formerly peaceful scene.

"Girl," Cara says, tossing the bags of blood at her, "where you been, who are you, and what did you do with our First Sister? Inquiring minds want to know." She says it as a joke, but there is half a bite to it.

Alice ignores it. Her clothes are askew and a little dirty, her hair a mess, her eyes dull and glassy, her skin extra pale—and not the cool, healthy vampire kind of pale.

Cara and I exchange *What the*—? looks and continue to quietly judge her.

She seems hard, tough, like she's been burning

the candle at both ends again.

Cara and I treat every mission like a campaign: a careful, considered, weeks-long journey toward a final destination. Alice sees everything as a sprint: get in, get the Vamplayer, get out. It's rarely that easy, but every time Alice forgets and thinks she can crack the case in seventy-two hours or less. I guess some Sisters never learn.

She ignores the straw that comes with every bag of blood, snaps her head back, releases her fangs, and drains it the old-fashioned way or, as Dr. Haskins would say, the rude way.

Watching Alice suck crudely at the plump plastic bag, siphoning off the platelets, the red rush, the slow burn, is a little like watching a hungry dog gnaw on a bone, growling a little, sniffing, snuffling, drooling, greedy: both are best left to their privacy.

I try to give her that privacy (and myself a break), but there's something different about the way Alice goes to town on the first bag and then, very quickly, the second. I just can't look away.

It happens so fast, and it's hard to tell anyway from this angle, but I could swear Alice's fangs look longer all of a sudden. I mean, okay, maybe it's an optical illusion, but they look *twice* as long as usual.

She seems greedier too, hungrier somehow than Cara and me combined. We've both gone without blood as long as she has, and Cara managed to suck lazily on her bags looking, if anything, elegant. And me? Well, I could have gone another day or two before getting really, truly blood hungry.

But here Alice is going to town like she hasn't been fed in weeks. Months, maybe. She finishes her bags, drops them to the floor—another no-no they teach us the first day at the Academy—and flops in the recliner with a satisfied belch. "Now that hit the spot."

I nudge her dirty bare feet off the coffee table. "What's gotten into you? You're not with your stupid friends anymore, so quit showing us how bad you can be. You're with your Sisters, remember? Drop the frat boy act, will ya?"

"Someone got up on the wrong side of the grave this morning, huh, Cara?" Alice says, avoiding eye contact with me and seeking support from her Second Sister.

She doesn't get it. "Make that two graves, Alice. Lily's right. Why are you suddenly acting the fool?"

Alice twirls around in her chair like a two-year-old full of sugar sitting on her first big girl barstool. "It's called acting, ladies, and maybe if you two did a little more of it, Bianca would accept you into her fold as well."

"Okay, fine," I say. "We applaud your ability to cozy up to Bianca so quickly, but let us know what's going on, all right? You staying out all night and dodging us all day is not okay."

"Yeah," Cara says, "where were you anyway?"

Alice smirks. "Nowhere special. The rugby team had a pool party, and Bianca thought it would be fun if I tagged along. That's all."

"A pool party?" I know I sound like a den mother but can't help myself. Does a gothic castle like Nightshade even have a pool, let alone parties?

"An *all-night* pool party?"

"An all-night, *naked* pool party. Only it wasn't a pool. There's this lake out behind the school. Unfortunately you couldn't see much in the murky waters, but I saw enough to know I can't wait for another all-night naked rugby team pool party."

"Fine, great," Cara says, and I can't tell if she's mad because Alice is being her usual reckless self or because she wasn't invited to skinny-dip with a bunch of thick necks. "We're really glad you've been accepted so quickly, but protocol states you need to check in every two hours or—"

"Protocol-schmotocol." Alice leaps out of the chair like a long-legged gymnast and disappears into her room. We hear her rifling through her drawers and closet, apparently for her third outfit of the day. "How am I supposed to check in every two hours when my phone is with the rest of my clothes a hundred yards away? This isn't about protocol, Cara. It's about politics, plain and simple."

"No," Cara says from the doorway, "it's about survival. What if one of those guys you were skinny-dipping with was the Vamplayer? What if he'd turned you or, worse, drained you? We didn't hear from you for nearly twelve hours. Alice, that's far too long to be safe."

I hear the familiar sound of metal hangers sliding across the rusty bar in her tiny closet.

"What if they'd gotten to you?" Cara says. "How would we even know?"

"How can we help you if we don't even know where you are?" I add, knowing I'm piling on, more concerned for Alice's safety than her feelings.

"Okay, okay." Alice still sounds unconvinced. "I'll call next time. Sheesh. Last I checked, you guys were supposed to be my Sisters, not my mothers."

There is a knock at the door.

Cara and I both freak, scrambling to gather one of the flattened blood sacks at Alice's feet like an empty beer can after a frat party.

"Are you expecting someone?" I say, tossing Dr. Haskins' special delivery box into my room.

The door swings open.

"Bianca, baby," Alice gushes, dramatically tossing a scarf around her bare shoulders and bounding from her room, nearly knocking Cara over in the process. She's wearing short shorts, a tube top, and wedge heels. (Hey, you can take the vampire out of the girl, but you can't take the girl out of the vampire.)

"Come on in!" she says unnecessarily.

Bianca's already middoorway by now. The nerve! She's wearing a sangria pencil skirt with a gold chain belt that cinches her size-two waist, a sheer white blouse with skinny arms over a black bra, and a severe black choker studded with rhinestones. It sounds gaudy and would be on most chicks, but Bianca works it something fierce.

I stand by my own doorway trying to look casual and note one last blood bag on the floor by Alice's easy chair. I shoot Cara a glance.

She spots it, quickly kicking it under the couch before Bianca can see it as well.

"This is cozy," Bianca says unconvincingly, slipping all the way into the suite and sliding the door shut behind her with a click that resonates with finality.

The way she says *cozy*, stretching it out into several syllables with a sneer (obviously her specialty), she makes it sound anything but.

"You've met my suite mates, Cara and Lily, haven't you?" Alice's tone is almost subservient, as if Bianca is some great-aunt with an even greater bank account and we're just scullery maids tidying up the place.

"If by *met* you mean *got slaughtered on the dodge-ball court*, then, yes, I've met them."

We all laugh.

Bianca rests her hand against a chair and waits while Alice finishes up in the bathroom. It's the first time we've been face-to-face without her nose all up in Tristan's armpit or her hands flinging dodge balls at me.

I can see why Tristan and Alice are enamored with her. It's not merely her flowing red hair, her angular pale face, her long elegant neck, or even longer sexier legs, to say nothing of her narrow waist and big boobs. Yes, she's got all the working parts. They're all fantastic and they all blend well together, but it's more than the sum of her parts. There's just something about her.

By the way Cara's checking her out, I can tell she can spot it too. We're not scoping her out in any type of official Sister capacity. This is purely girl stuff.

Whatever Bianca has going for her, it's working. I can't put a name on it, exactly, other than to say it's pretty powerful stuff. It's something the "it girls" in every school have. And trust me, we've seen and saved hundreds by now. It's not that they're the most beautiful, though Bianca is certainly gorgeous, but there are dozens of girls who are, say, hotter. They might have longer legs, better abs, more striking eyes or cheekbones. But they lack her presence, her command of a room, her strength of personality.

I can see why Tristan chose her, why he's seducing her, and why of all the girls at Nightshade it's Bianca he'll try to turn into a Vampress. She has what he needs: access. She has the connections, the friends, the parties, the hookups, the influence, and of course the respect of just about everybody at Nightshade. Everybody who counts, anyway.

Once Tristan turns her, tells her what he needs from her, it will be nothing for her to turn the rest of the school, regardless of what she's selling. If a girl like Bianca says, "Hey, gang, we're going to an all-night rave in this abandoned barn and the only price of admission is that I have to bite your neck on the way in," forget about it. It would be standing-room-only vampires in ten minutes or less.

That's why our job as Sisters isn't merely to spot the Vamplayer but to identify his likely victim. If we can get to her, make her see what's going on, even keep her out of harm's way, then the Vamplayer usually gives up, calls it a draw, and moves on.

I just hope we'll be able to stop him in time.

Alice sprays more perfume than should be humanly possible onto her radiant throat.

"So," I say like the older sister who's already in her nightgown at eight and looking forward to a hot cup of tea and a good book by the fire while the younger one races around getting ready to use her fake ID at some bar downtown, "what are you two doing tonight?"

Bianca looks at Alice and then Cara. "Not much," she answers without looking at me, apparently admiring Cara's mocha skin and long, black braids. "But we were hoping *you* could join us."

The sudden attention seems to both embarrass and flatter Cara.

It's such a small room, and so much is going on. I can see it all in slow motion, like with the dodge balls earlier, gelling together in this prep-school-rich-witch-mean-girls-bad-eighties-movie way. I'm being left behind even as I'm compelled to watch the train departing from the station without me.

Cara in particular seems caught up in a whirl-wind of emotions. I can see them cross her face. She's obviously thinking about what's best for the Academy, for Dr. Haskins, for the mission, then pouting and thinking about what's best for her—even for me.

She's not answering, so I answer for us. "Well, that all depends. There's that term paper due tomorrow and—"

"I meant Cara," Bianca snaps, interrupting me.

No, not just interrupting me. Silencing me.

I stand stock still.

Cara avoids looking at me. "M-m-me?" she stammers like the fat kid on the softball field who can't believe he's been picked first instead of last for a team.

"Of course." Bianca draws closer to my Second Sister. "I've been admiring you since you got here. And I couldn't help but notice how the cheerleaders have cozied up to you. Nice going, by the way. They're a pretty frosty bunch. And, of course, that's fine. Better to hang with the cheerleaders than the losers some of you have fallen in with." Here, with her emerald-green eyes, she chews me up and spits me out. "But Tristan and I were talking, and Alice agrees it might be time for an upgrade in the friends department for you, Cara. What do you say?"

There is no time for me to argue, intercede, or even breathe.

"I-i-if you think it's a good idea, Bianca."

"Oh, she does, she does." Alice scoots them both out the door before I can protest too loudly—or at all.

Cara moves hastily, decision made, her long, straight back to me. She grabs her purse off her doorknob and rushes to Bianca's side as if she thinks this one-time offer might quickly expire.

Alice swings the door almost shut, stopping short to look at me. Smiling—no, sneering—she says, "Don't wait up. This could be another all-nighter."

CHAPTER 13

A lice's words prove prophetic. Cara doesn't come back to the dorm that night. But then, neither does Alice.

I get some rest, just enough to be vital in case anything shakes loose the next day. The small, metal bed squeaks every time I move. I wake myself out of a finicky sleep, look at the clock on my bare wooden nightstand, and know there's no use even trying anymore.

My running shoes are on the floor, under the window, beckoning me to join Tristan for another early morning run. I stand, stretch, reach for them, then think better of it.

Do I really want to go there?

Today?

Instead, I pace the floors in the dark, hearing them creak beneath me, roaming in and out of my Sister's empty rooms, imagining them walking in at that very moment, seeing me, hugging me, explaining to me, making me understand, reassuring me. Isn't that what Sisters are for?

It's lonely here in these four silent rooms, this grim building groaning, shivering around me.

Light from a streetlamp four stories down filters through the cheap, drawn curtains. I'm tempted to peer out, searching for Alice, for Cara, but know I won't find them. Not that way. And certainly not down there.

I pause in the center of the room, restless, tired, frustrated, and fearful, and think of the mission, of how it's going.

Of how it's going wrong.

Yes, it's our job to infiltrate the in-crowd, to go undercover, to win their hearts and minds, all so the Vamplayer can't get to them first.

But this is all moving a little too fast. It's going a little too well.

I know I shouldn't complain, but I can't help it. Something feels off. Anyone who's ever shown up at a new school, especially a cloistered one like Night-shade, knows you're not going to get accepted, let alone embraced, overnight.

It usually takes time for the new girls to be accepted, especially when those girls aren't really girls at all. A week for us to feel the place out, another to find our niches, one more to make our moves, another to prove ourselves, a final one for the popular crowd to accept us, and then we're in.

The longest it's ever taken is two months.

The shortest was two weeks.

But two days?

I dunno, something smells fishy here at Night-shade, and the thought of exchanging barbs with Tristan all morning as we try to outdo each other on the track literally turns my stomach.

That's the hardest part about being a Sister. Yes, the drama sucks major, but it's something I'm used to. What really rubs me the wrong way is being so close to a Vamplayer and wanting to rip his fangs out but having to play nice.

"Oh, you look so good today, Tristan. Did you get a haircut? Have you been working out?" When all I really want to say is, "Hey, Tristan, how do you want your stake this morning? From the front through the rib cage or from behind through the spine?"

I mean, it's enough to turn a girl schizo if she's not careful.

Okay, Lily. I quietly count to ten. *Go to your happy place!*

Suddenly I picture Zander's face when I bumped into him yesterday morning, so confused, so hurt. I picture his apron, slung casually over his bony shoulder for another long day at work.

I look at the clock and get a better idea.

CHAPTER 14

The cafeteria is empty, dreary, and smells faintly of bleach, but the kitchen is already humming when I arrive at the red double doors dressed in my loose jeans, sneakers, and long-sleeved gray T-shirt tight enough to impress but loose enough to move around in.

Grover sees me first, his already mussed hair frizzy from the stifling kitchen heat.

I press one finger to my lips and point to Zander.

Grover smiles, nods, and returns to scrubbing dried egg off the biggest frying pan I've ever seen in my life.

The kitchen seems small and cramped to feed so

many so fast, but right now it's just the three of us and feels oddly intimate.

I tread quietly across the slippery rust-colored tiles, careful to avoid a big shiny steel table where knives and towering bowls threaten to topple at the lightest tap.

Zander is standing in the doorway of the chilly walk-in cooler opening up crates marked *lettuce* when I sneak up from behind and tap him lightly on the shoulder.

"Hi, Lily," he says with an exaggerated yawn, his fingertips covered in lettuce juice.

"How did you know?" I'm glad Dr. Haskins isn't around to see how quickly I've forgotten my sneaking-up-on-humans tactics.

He points to the shiny inside of the walk-in door, where even now I can see my pale reflection. (Vampires only deny their reflection when they're in full-on vamp mode, you know, in case you're keeping track of that kind of thing.)

I grin, slug his shoulder, and reach for an apron hanging off a nearby hook on the white-tiled wall. "So, I came to help. What can I do?"

Grover joins us, the bottom of his too-small Cookie Monster T-shirt peeking over his large, pale belly.

They look at each other and ask, "Why?"

I shrug. "I'm here. Does it really matter why?"

Grover shrugs, which draws his shirt up even more to expose a Lucky Charms belt buckle straining across the top of his dark blue cords.

Zander frowns. "What, your boy toy stand you up at the track this morning?" His voice is warm, but his gaze is cool.

"He's not my boy toy."

"Hmmm." He snorts, bending back to his lettuce. "It sure looked like it when I surprised you both yesterday morning."

"What? When? Why do I miss all the good stuff?" Grover asks good-naturedly.

"Well, if you'd gotten up when I tried to drag your big carcass out of bed yesterday morning, you would have been with me to see Lily and her new squeeze, Tristan, toweling each other off by the track."

"What? I never—"

Zander smiles. "Okay, Grover, maybe they weren't toweling each other off, but they still looked pretty darn cozy to me."

Grover looks skeptical. "I didn't know the track was where all the pretty people went to pick up all the other pretty people nowadays." He sucks in his gut and pounds his chest, King Kong–style. "Maybe I'll dust off the old Reeboks and give it a whirl tomorrow morning."

"Well, why wait?" I say. "I bet Tristan's out there right now, running by his lonesome since I stood him up to hang around the kitchen with you two. Suddenly I'm rethinking my decision."

"Oh, playing hard to get, are we?" Zander says.

I purse my lips and try not to clench my fists. "It's pretty hard to play hard to get when nothing's going on in the first place."

"If you say so." He sighs, stretching his back.

Grover sees the fire between us and retreats to the dishwasher, which is noisy enough to drown out our major drama moment.

I wait until the hose is hissing away, turn to Zander with both hands on my hips, and say, "It didn't look like anything *because nothing was going on.*"

His hands are on his hips, and beneath his apron he's doing the snug jeans and tight white T-shirt thing. His high-tops are stained with lettuce drippings and ketchup. His curls are flatter than usual, and I instantly think bedhead but in a kind of good way. He smiles crookedly. "It sure looked like it to me."

"Well, then you have a dirty mind. Is that my fault?"

He shoves me playfully. "Only when I picture

you soaking wet in my bathroom."

"What?"

"Oh, wait, that came out wrong."

"Yeah." I slug him. "Try *real* wrong."

"What I meant was, well, it was a play on words, actually." His face is red and getting redder. "Bathrooms are dirty, and yesterday when we soaked you with the hose, you were soaking wet and . . . oh, forget it. I guess I'm not as smooth as Tristan."

I shake my head. "I came here to help, not to fight with you."

He winks. "I'm just messing with you."

"No, you're not."

"Yeah, you're right, but I don't want to fight either."

"Let's work instead."

Come to find out, Zander isn't just stacking lettuce boxes after all. He's peeling off the top, skuzzy layer of leaves so when the cooks come in later this morning to prep for lunch, they won't have to.

He teaches me how to do it. I literally haven't held a head of lettuce, let alone eaten one, since the eighties. He shows me where to toss the outer layer, and we settle into a steady groove.

"How much lettuce do the kids here eat?" I ask after my third box of three dozen heads of lettuce.

He snickers. "It's not that the kids eat so much lettuce. It's that there are so many kids. Now keep peeling!"

Meanwhile, from time to time, Grover taps out some random tune on the bottom of a pot he's just cleaned before he hangs it up to dry. At the moment it's the theme from *Halloween*.

"Have you two always been friends?"

He winces at the constant pot battering. "Who says we're friends?"

I give him some time, peel one more box of lettuce, and reach for another.

"He's from Boston originally." Zander looks at Grover, who's deep into cleaning another pan, before continuing. "He showed up halfway through freshman year angry— and why not? He'd just gotten kicked out of another prep school, some dump down in Florida, showed up in our dorm suite huffing and puffing. It just so happened I was ditching class on account of a *Battlestar Galactica* marathon that was running all day, all night. He sat down, grabbed the popcorn, and I've been his nursemaid ever since." He smiles in a bittersweet, almost wistful, *what my life might have been without Grover* way.

"So you tamed the savage beast, huh?" I smirk, if only to lighten the mood, and toss a lettuce leaf at him.

He deflects it and laughs. "Something like that."

"Why'd his parents send him away in the first place?"

He shrugs. "They're uptight preppies who never understood him. He took me home that first Christmas. You know, to show his folks he'd finally made a 'normal' friend, whatever that means. They've got this huge brownstone on one of the nicest streets in Boston. His mom's in an apron, one of those frilly lace things like French maids wear, cooking dinner when we come in. Dad's at the bar—yes, they have a bar in their house—with Grover's older brother. They're both in slacks, starched white shirts, and suspenders. Here come Grover and I fresh from the train, high off his Laffy Taffy stash, in matching Freddy Krueger T-shirts. They take one look at us, and we spend the rest of the holiday playing video games in the basement. Needless to say, we haven't been invited back."

"We?"

He shrugs again. "Grover hasn't been home since."

"Well, what do you guys do for holidays, spring break, summer?"

He holds up two heads of lettuce. "You're looking at it."

I grin. "Please tell me your story's slightly less tragic."

He shakes his head. "You first."

"What, me? What about me?"

"Well, for starters, what's up with you and your friends? Most girls don't show up to Nightshade with a built-in posse, you know?"

I shrug and rattle off the same old lines we've long since memorized as our cover story. "We're from the same town in Florida, Catfish Cove. No? Never heard of it? Anyway, our folks are a lot like Grover's: rich, bored, and selfish. We got sent away freshman year and get shipped around from school to school. New York for a year. LA for another. Now here we are."

"Yeah, but why together? I mean, how? Nightshade's pretty hard to get into for one troubled kid at a time, let alone three at the same time."

"What?" I snap, eager to go off script and quit lying. "I'm troubled?"

He slaps me a lettuce five. "You know what I mean."

"Well, let's just say we promised our folks if we can't all go away to school together, we're all coming home together. I guess it's important enough for them to keep us away from home that they work their magic." I rub my fingertips together. "Money talks."

"I wouldn't know. Why do you think I'm doing this?"

"Hey." I bump him with my hip as he reaches for a fresh box of lettuce. "I'm doing this too."

"Yeah, but you're volunteering. You don't have to do it. Grover and I do."

"So how come?" I ask. "I mean, how come you're here, doing this?"

After a shrug and a peek at Grover, he says, "I got in some trouble in junior high. Nothing major but enough to get sent away. My dad couldn't deal. Some guy at work told him about this place. I've been here ever since."

I shake my head. "That doesn't sound like you. The 'trouble' part, I mean."

Another shrug. "They said I was acting out after my mom left. I say I was bored."

"What, you hadn't discovered sci-fi yet?"

He smiles, biting his lower lip. "Pretty much."

"So, what, you stick around holidays and summers to keep Grover company? That's a pretty good friend."

"Yeah, well, I'm in no rush to go home either. Trust

me. Dad's new wife makes those Real Housewives look like Mother Teresa, if you know what I mean."

Only a few boxes of lettuce remain. Both of us slow down. Me, to stretch out our time together. Him, I dunno. Maybe that's why he does it too.

We grow quiet, peaceful, closer.

His warm elbow bumps mine. He works on the lettuce carefully, methodically. When he's done stripping off the leafy, dirty outer layer, what's left is grocery store commercial smooth and clean while mine look like the blooper reel versions. I can't help it: his hands are intoxicating, the long fingers thin but strong and nimble. His wrists are agile and lean, his sleek forearm muscles flexing like pistons as he slowly but surely moves through another box of lettuce.

The kitchen grows even smaller around us, the constant sound of Grover's hissing hose gun like one of those rainforest CDs in the background, lulling us into lettuce-peeling, leaning-into-each-other pod people.

"Thanks," he says, breaking my reverie, which involves my clothes being peeled like a head of lettuce by Zander's long, tender fingers.

"Who-how-why-wuzzthat?" I mumble dreamily, looking up into his deep hazel twinkling eyes.

He snorts. "Thanks. I mean, for coming in today."

"I was probably more trouble than I was worth."

"Pretty much." He nods to the many dozens of lettuce leaves I've over- or undershot at the trash can. "But as far as hired help goes, you're a lot prettier to look at than my usual partner."

"Hey!" Grover spurts the hose at our feet to get our attention.

It works.

We jump, scattering lettuce leaves and toppling the final, empty box.

"Speaking of partners, it just so happens there's a zombie marathon on the Scream Channel tonight." Grover looks at me. "Whaddya say, partner?"

"What?" Suddenly I'm feeling like the poor relations. "Our suite doesn't even have a TV, let alone cable."

"Yeah, well, rank has its privileges. You game?"

I hesitate, looking to Zander for some sign whether this is a good or bad idea. I think of Alice and Cara, not to mention Bianca, and another lonely night in the dorm.

"All the Laffy Taffy you can eat," Grover says, literally sweetening the deal.

I slug the big guy, feeling more muscle than fat.

He pretends to nurse his wound.

"Oh, silly." I bat my eyelashes and clasp my hands dramatically at my bosom Southern belle–style. "You had me at zombie."

Fortunately, Grover's not the only one smiling at my reply.

O h, what a difference a day makes. Yesterday, PE was a little slice of heaven. Today, it's hell on earth. Apparently, once a month a nurse from the local hospital comes in to teach something called Feminine Hygiene Systems and Maintenance. (Yeah, that's what *I* thought.)

Anyway, so while Zander, Grover, and Tristan are out playing pickup soccer with the rest of the boys, we girls get to sit in a spare classroom next to the gym and watch a slide show about how to avoid and treat yeast infections. (Yummy.)

The day started off rocky and has gone downhill. For starters, I haven't seen Cara and Alice since last night.

They weren't in the dorm suite after my voluntary KP duty this morning. I got ready alone. I went to my first class alone, second class alone, and so on.

I saw them in the halls, so I knew they were safe, but they were always either with Bianca or racing to catch up with her. There was no time to connect.

Now here we are in the same classroom but miles apart.

As we settle into our seats in clusters, Mrs. Moxley greets us with a smile. She's wearing simple white slacks, comfortable white shoes, and one of those Garfield nurse smocks with the wide pockets over the hips.

Alice and Cara steer clear of me. That's fine. I get it. It's all a job. Still, I came in as part of a group that's now fractured, and the other girls in the school don't know what to do with me. Should they rally around, patting me on the shoulders, or stay away in case Bianca catches them and practices a little guilt by association? Apparently they vote in favor of steering clear, so there I sit, front row and center, my neck hot, my shoulders tense. It seems like the entire class is whispering behind my back.

The slide show is torturous: twenty-eight screens of various close-ups of female anatomy better not discussed here. Suffice it to say I now have an honorary degree in gynecology, whether I wanted one or not. (For the record, I didn't.)

The spitballs start around slide seventeen. One at first, landing just so on the empty desk next to me. Another to my left. Tightly rolled and expertly lubricated, it sticks to the empty seat and doesn't budge, even when I try to flick it away so nobody will see. Yeah right. I'm in the front row. I might as well be wearing a bull's-eye on my back.

By slide nineteen I can feel two on my shoulder, one on my arm. I shake them off, cringing with disgust.

The twittering builds softly, one row back, then left, then right, then the row after that. By slide twenty-two, it's like a wave that crests, then ebbs. I'm hopeful every time the rolling whitewash of laughter rolls out to sea, only to be disappointed moments later when it begins all over again.

The nurse at the front of the class is clueless, apparently assuming we're all just nervous and giggling at the slides of women's anatomy.

She couldn't be any more wrong.

I couldn't be any more desperate.

Finally the show is over, and before the lights go on I quickly try to dislodge the spit wads from my hair, blanching with each handful. The floor beneath my desk is littered with my castoffs, and still I feel them sticking to the small of my back.

I wish for a shower or at least a bathroom run, but I dare not raise my hand for fear of drawing even more attention—and another volley of spitballs—to myself.

And still it's far from over.

"Now that you know what to look for, ladies, I'd like you to pair up and discuss how you might tell a BFF if you suspect she's harboring one of our nasty little friends here," Mrs. Moxley says, sending a stake of fear right through my heart.

I scramble, looking for a kind face, seeing only the backs of heads or downcast eyes.

"We don't have much time, and I don't want to turn this into a popularity contest, so I'll pick teams."

I'm silently thanking her for saving my day until she seats me with none other than—you guessed it—Bianca Ridley.

"Uh, Mrs. Moxley, I think the girl you paired me with has a spitball infection," she says, pointing to some paper and saliva mass in the middle of my back.

Giggles explode around the room.

"Now, now, girls, you have your pairs. Get to work."

Alice and Cara have been grouped together,

naturally, but Mrs. Moxley seats them in a corner of their own. Bianca isn't coming to me, so I have to walk all the way to her, passing them on the way. "Thanks."

Cara looks mildly ashamed, but there's something else in her eyes. A distance. No, that's not quite right.

A coldness. And something else. A darkness lurking there. Cara's eyes have always been alive, happy, but now her gaze is tense like she's hiding something.

Something big. Something even she doesn't want to admit to.

As First Sister Alice is usually carefree, laughing, not caring about me or even Cara all that much. She's always just getting her share and eager to report back to Dr. Haskins as soon as she can.

But now she too seems wary. Docile, even.

They keep looking past me to Bianca.

I step in between them, just for spite, and stomp over to my partner. "So," I say glumly, slumping into a desk facing Bianca, "what are we supposed to do?"

"Who cares? I'm not even talking to you until you get cleaned up anyway."

"Well, Bianca, how am I supposed to do that?"

"How am I to know, Lily? But it's unsanitary, to say the least."

"You should have thought of that before you peppered me with spitballs."

She crosses her bare arms, shifting her body encased in a tight chocolate-brown dress with matching heels. "I'm sure I don't know what you're talking about."

"I'm talking about a high school junior who throws spitballs like a freshman. No, like a *middle schooler*."

She swipes an auburn lock behind one pale ear. "Maybe you should get the hint, Lily. Then nobody will need to shoot spit wads at you."

I don't take the bait. I don't have to. I've been here six hundred times before.

Why is the girl we're supposed to protect from the Vamplayer always, *always*, inevitably the Head Witch in Charge?

Just once can't we rescue a nice, kind, empathetic, worthy, cool chick who would actually, you know, appreciate it?

I slink down across from her, my hands tightly gripping my desk. I could snap her neck with my pinkie, but I'm unable to do anything at the moment.

She seems content to be silent, which is of course how I prefer her, so I slouch and glare at Alice and Cara instead.

They ignore me and even Bianca, looking intently at each other, whispering across the two desks they've pushed together. No, it's not whispering; it's more like hissing. And I mean real hissing. Like Komodo dragon hissing.

"What'd you do to my friends?" I say, not looking at Bianca.

"They look *fine* to me," she says proudly, as if she had anything to do with it.

We're both leaning back now, our elbows at our sides, our backs halfway down the chairs, our knees almost touching.

How she manages to look elegant in that dress and at the same time comfortable in a slouch is beyond me, but I guess that's why Tristan loves her.

"Fine? Are you kidding me? They look like zombies. Look at Cara. She hasn't smiled all period. And that girl is normally addicted to smiling."

Bianca corrects me. "She smiled when your hair was filling up with spitballs. I know that much."

"Whatever. And Alice? I haven't seen her this sad since *21 Jump Street* went off the air."

Oops. Big slip.

Big slip.

"What's that?"

Obviously, Bianca is clueless about the minor eighties TV drama that launched Johnny Depp's career.

"Inside joke." I squirm in my seat. How could I be so stupid?

Luckily, despite Bianca's obvious charms, brain-power is not one of them.

"Whatever." She sighs, admiring her nails. "I don't see you spending a ton of time with your *sisters* this semester, do you?"

"Do *you*?" I snap, wondering if she suspects something about Alice, Cara, and me or if *Sisters* is just her fancy way of saying *friends*, *girls*, whatever.

She shrugs. "Sure, why not? They're fun to be around."

I see Cara's grim expression, her unkempt hair, and last night's red jeans. "They don't look so fun right now."

"Maybe you're sitting too close to them."

I regard her carefully. "What is it about certain girls that they can't share friends—that they have to take friends instead?"

"If they were really your friends, do you think I could take them away from you so easily?"

I smile. "Is that how you do it? Is that your shtick? You talk me down to build yourself up?"

She shifts in her seat. "It doesn't take much talking when it comes to you, Lily. It's clear you don't belong here."

I stare her down. "I'm not going anywhere."

She shrugs. "We'll see about that."

The bell rings, and I stand, eager to do something, tear something, trip something, break something.

As if we've been politely chitchatting, Bianca stands gracefully, straightens the front of her dress, and walks directly to Alice and Cara.

They rise slowly to greet her. Well, at least Alice does. Cara needs some help, which Bianca and Alice give her, if begrudgingly. She looks weak. Like, blood weak.

But she fed last night, same as me.

Still, her shoulders are slumped, her eyes glazed, her skin ashy and clammy.

If I didn't know better, I'd say she was . . . turning.

But that's impossible. Vampires don't turn, do they?

As they lean to help her, Cara shoots me a look. In it are our many years of friendship, a wink of compassion, and maybe an ounce of regret. For her? For me? It happens so fast, it's hard to tell.

Then she blinks, and the look is gone. In its place is another: anger, fear, anxiety, even confusion. It's the look of a wounded animal with its leg stuck in a trap, panicking half the time, denying the hopelessness of its situation the rest, alternating between pain and sadness, victory and defeat, hope and hopelessness.

I've never seen that look before. I'm quite certain I never want to see it again.

Now she's up, and the girls are helping her across the room, out the door, and into the crowded hallways, where they're absorbed like blood into the stream.

I want to follow, but it's no use.

With Bianca around, there's no talking to Alice and Cara.

I begin the long walk to my next class. It feels more like an ending.

CHAPTER 16

I sit alone at dinner that night, sour and anxious after another long day. Alice and Cara are nowhere to be found, MIA since PE (so much for Cara's big protocol speech last night). I feel self-conscious after the spitball incident, aware that many more eyes than usual are looking my way and none for the right reasons. At least I'm clean now, double-showered and changed, but I still feel slightly dirty and plenty betrayed.

Zander and Grover are hustling around. I try to help them again, images of peeling lettuce and other things with Zander all night dancing around in my head. But their scruffy kitchen manager, a guy by the name of Palermo (though he looks more Irish than Italian) kicks me out of the kitchen on account of liability issues.

So here I am, alone in a sea of happy faces.

A finger taps my shoulder.

I smile, expecting to see Grover's chubby cheeks or Zander's crooked smile.

Instead I see Tristan sliding out a chair next to me, his tray full of fruit cups and cottage cheese. "Is this seat taken?" he asks knowingly, already sitting down, as if I could kick him out even if I wanted to.

"Not tonight." I shrug, pushing around a few hush puppies on my plate for good measure. "My suite mates are MIA."

"No, they're not," he says quietly, poking open an apple juice box but not taking a sip. "They're with Bianca and the girls, the rugby team, and a few other various jock types down at the Burger Barn in Ravens Roost."

"What? Isn't that like a twenty-five-minute drive? What'd they do? Fly?"

"Hardly. Bianca has a car. The rugby team has a van. They do let students drive where you come from, don't they?"

"Yeah. I just didn't think they did here at Nightshade."

He grunts. "Too right, but in case you haven't noticed, Bianca has a certain way of charming people."

"Tell me about it." I picture Cara's face the night before in our dorm room, practically beaming at the thought of spending a night in Bianca's holy presence. "I just don't take Headmistress Holly as the easily charmed type, if you know what I mean."

"Indeed, I do. And she isn't, but what Headmistress Holly doesn't know won't hurt her, right?"

I shrug, break up a hush puppy with my fork, and move it around some more.

The chatter in the cafeteria builds. I try to ignore the whispers and fingers pointed in our direction.

"I missed you at the track this morning," he says through tight lips, considering a piece of overripe watermelon on his fork before putting it back on his plate. "I thought we had a deal."

"Did we?" I watch from across the room as Zander labors under another heavy bus tray. "I thought I made it pretty clear I'd show up when I felt like it."

He arches his eyebrows. "I see." He sounds vaguely like Bianca with his superior, sarcastic tone. "From the way you were lapping me yesterday, I thought you felt a whole *lot* like it."

I swallow a rebuke because it's not my job to feel; it's my job to pretend. I shrug, bite off a frown, and quip, "Well, somebody has to play hard to get around here."

He laughs uproariously, enough to draw the attention of students at several nearby tables, including Zander, who quickly disappears behind the kitchen door. "I must admit you're a far sight frostier than your suite mates. What are their names again? Malice and Farah?"

I laugh. Despite his massive ego and obvious Vamplayer tendencies, Tristan does have a certain charm about him. It's equal parts aloof and knowing, confident and condescending. It says, *Aren't I special? Aren't you lucky I'm talking to you? Don't you dare think of not falling in love with me.* It wouldn't normally appeal to me, this blatant cockiness, but for some reason Tristan wears it well. Very well.

"It's Alice and Cara," I correct him, trying to sound equally haughty and failing. "You might want to know the names of the girls you go skinny-dipping with."

He looks at me, opens his mouth to say something, then shuts it, playing with his cottage cheese until the lumps are lumpier and the whole thing is runny.

"Alice," he says deliberately, his thin lips caressing the letters. "Cara. Yes, I'll have to remember that next time we are, how do you say, skinny-dipping?"

"Don't be such a prude," I say as the heat of his body wafts over like an expensive cologne. "I doubt you're unfamiliar with the term."

He shakes his head, smiles, and with no trace of irony says, "If you'd care to show me, I'd certainly be more than happy to—"

"Oh, no." I laugh, nudging him with my shoulder. "Like you said, I'm the frosty one."

He overturns another spoonful of cottage cheese. I swear he hasn't taken one bite. "Frosty? Did I really say you were frosty?"

I can't pin down his accent. It's not entirely European, like that of some of the students whose rich foreign parents obviously ship them here to Nightshade for an exceptional education, but there are a few traces. It's more adult than anything, be it his word choices—*indeed, certainly*—or the way he seems to measure every word like they all matter.

"Yes, yes, you did. Just ten seconds ago you called me the frosty one."

"Oh dear, that's not very complimentary, is it?"

I shake my head. "No, in fact. And I demand an

apology, or I'll have security roust you out of that chair in no time."

Good gawd, am I? Am I really?

Yes, I am. I'm actually *flirting* with this creep.

Suddenly I feel bad about judging Alice and Cara for falling under Bianca's spell so easily and so soon. Ten words and two smiles from Tristan, and I'm all soupy like his room temperature cottage cheese.

"This?" he says, pointing to the kitchen doors where Grover and Zander scowl in our general direction until they see us looking and duck through the swinging doors. "This is your idea of security?"

I don't know if he recognizes Zander from bumping into him after our run yesterday morning or is simply disparaging all kitchen help as a group (probably), but I don't respond.

We sit in awkward silence until he puts his hand flat over mine and says, "You're right. I do owe you an apology. And I would like to make it privately, if you don't mind."

His hand is warm and, before I know it, he's pulled me up from my seat and is walking me through the cafeteria. I don't resist; it's like I *can't* resist. And it's not just any old walk. This guy is known for making grand entrances. Why would his exits be any less grand? He has my hand in the crook of his arm, like we're prom king and queen. His pace is steady and measured, like he's done this a thousand times before.

I just want to bolt before Grover and Zander see us leaving together.

A hush falls in the room, and Tristan guides me past what seem like miles of gawking faces, all of them whispering, most of them, "Bianca," until at last we are on the other side of the cafeteria doors and I have the presence of mind to stop him.

"Hold on. Hold *on*. Who are you and what did you do with that big snob Tristan?"

He smiles, kissing me before I can stop him.

And long after I can stop him.

CHAPTER 17

Tristan's room is a few floors up from mine, but we stop there for only a moment. He walks into his dorm suite, and through the barely cracked door I hear some muted TV show. (Does everyone have a TV but us?)

When he emerges, he has a picnic basket in his hand.

"What?" I snort, disbelieving. "You happened to have a picnic basket within reach of your front door?"

He grins. "A gentleman must always be prepared."

"Prepared for what? We just ate!"

"You call that swill back there food?" he huffs.

He leads me down the stairs, through a back

hallway, out across a small employee parking lot behind the school, and toward a secluded spot in the deserted faculty break area. We're just close enough to the school to feel safe, whatever *that* feels like, but far enough away from the rest of the cafeteria clowns or after-dinner jocks on the rugby field to have privacy.

The sun has set by now, the night is cool, and I'm glad I chose to dress modestly for dinner in fluted slacks and a beaded sweater.

He finds us a stone picnic table, the kind no one ever really sits at, and places the heavy wicker basket on top. He dusts off my seat dramatically and invites me to sit across from him. His actions and very presence make me feel like I'm at the nicest French restaurant in town.

Stupid Vamplayers. Why do they always have to be so damn charming?

As if on cue, the encroaching darkness signals a porch light next to the faculty break area to flicker to life; we both blink in its sudden brightness.

He takes off his leather jacket, the weathered charcoal kind with two tan stripes down the arms, and wraps it around my shoulders. It's like something out of some romcom Alice would watch four thousand times and Cara and I would make fun of four thousand one times.

"But you'll freeze to death," I say before I can stop myself (total romcom line if I've ever heard one).

He points to the gray hoodie he had on underneath. "Like I said, a gentleman always comes prepared." He sits and opens the basket.

Immediately my senses are awash with a bouquet of pleasing scents, which is strange because I never, ever lust for human food.

Then again, this isn't human food. At least, not in the strictest sense of the word. I can sense the ripe blood before I even see it, before I even smell it.

"Blood cheese," he says quietly, almost reverently, unwrapping a thick wedge of the imported delicacy.

My hunger is so strong it's all I can do to not snatch it out of his hand and devour it, fangs out, before his very eyes, mission be damned.

"Blood sausage." He slides another foil-wrapped package onto the picnic table. "Chilled blood consommé and, for dessert, blood wine. She even sent plastic glasses, two of them, as if she knew—"

"She who?"

"Why, Mother of course." (He may as well have added, *Ta-da!*)

I shrug. That's good enough for me. The hunger is too potent for me to be suspicious.

We gorge ourselves. Well, mostly I gorge myself.

The blood cheese is heavenly, heavy on the blood, light on the cheese, and literally melting the minute it hits my tongue and evaporating into my system the way a tea bag bleeds in hot water.

The blood sausage is richer but no less fulfilling as my thirsty cells drink up every last drop of its rich, oily goodness, no need for digestion of any kind.

And the blood wine is quite literally intoxicating.

"Oh, I haven't had this in years." I'm so ecstatic I almost say, *Decades!*

Pump the brakes, Lily. Pump 'em! Don't let a little thing like blood wine sabotage the whole mission.

"Really? We have it all the time where I come from."

I bet you do, I think but don't say. Best to let him do all the talking. Despite the quasi-romantic setting and extravagant meal, I'm still at work. This is still an interrogation. "I've never met anyone like you," I say, like they taught me in Advanced Vamp-layer Flirting.

I lean closer, lips flush and thick from the intake of blood, senses on high alert, pores open, fangs quivering below the gum line, making my teeth tingle.

"Nor you I," he says eloquently (I think), and I practically need a dictionary to decipher it. "You are like a flower, Lily, in more than name."

Wow, he is good.

I don't need a dictionary to translate his next move. One hand creeps into the leather jacket and straight toward my chest.

I slap it briskly, so sated by the meal, so super-charged I think I hear something snap.

"Witch," he says, standing, clutching his offending hand close to his chest. "After all I've done for you. This meal. Do you know how much it cost to import to this godforsaken school in these godforsaken sticks? I think I deserve a little—"

A sound behind us interrupts him, which is good because if he'd said two more words my foot would've interrupted him one way or the other—although he still would have been able to talk, if you know what I mean.

He sniffs, grabs his precious wicker basket plus the rest of the blood wine, and stomps off.

"We're not through here," he says over his shoulder before disappearing into the school.

"Trust me," I say to the breeze rustling the branches in the tree line. "I know."

CHAPTER 18

I am not alone in the dark.

It isn't just the breeze rustling the branches.

Three figures emerge from the tree line just beyond the picnic area, looking gaunt and ghostly in the darkness surrounding them.

It's such an odd sight, like something you'd see in a really bad scary movie, that it takes me a minute to focus. When I do, the words pour out of my mouth: "Bianca? Alice? Cara?"

They step forward, as if they've choreographed the whole scene to look extra super creepy, then stand there looking at me.

And looking.

And watching.

And waiting.

They don't say a word. Not one. Not to me, not to each other. This from two girls who have not shut up in the entire time I've known them.

I stand but stay put. I know it's stupid, especially for me, but it feels safer somehow on the patio under the lights.

"What are you guys doing?" My voice disappears into the darkness once it's past the cloistered little patio area where we've been enjoying our picnic. You know, until Mr. Vamplayer got all touchy-feely at the last minute.

"Aren't you cold, standing out there?" I say, realizing I'm still wearing Tristan's jacket. I tug it closer around me, feeling his warmth lingering in the shoulders, on my arms. It smells vaguely of cigarettes and imported cologne.

Nothing.

They don't even blink.

They look eerie, odd.

For girls who are normally so active to suddenly just be standing there, doing nothing—I think that's the scariest part of all.

I move to the left, positioning myself for a run at

the back hallway door.

Only then do they move, advancing in unison two full footsteps.

"Guys, come on, you're freaking me out. It's late. Are you kidding me with this?"

I sound so corny speaking to the wind, talking to spirits, but it's like the quieter they are, the more I want to talk.

They shake their heads, again in synchrony, and take two steps forward into the light of the patio.

I see Cara's fangs first and am immediately upset that she'd bare them in front of Bianca like this. Revealing herself to a civilian so blatantly? And soon?

Protocol, my butt. That's it. I'm writing her up when we get to the Academy. Her and Alice both. I don't care if they do outrank me.

This whole assignment has been strictly amateur hour. I don't blame Dr. Haskins for keeping us out of the Saviors if this is how we're going to—

Cara's fangs! They're twice as long as I've ever seen them, and she's well past the age when her fangs should have stopped growing.

Alice's too. She smiles next to Cara, and her fangs just keep extending past the point where they usually stop.

It's like they've gotten fang extensions in the last forty-eight hours.

A kind of secret ripple passes among them, and they smile. The fangs retract, if they were ever out in the first place. Am I seeing things out here in the moonlight?

"Lily?" Cara says, "What are you doing here?" Her tone is vaguely accusatory, like I've caught her up to something rather than the other way around.

"Me? What are you guys doing out there? Just lurking. You nearly scared me half to death."

"Oh, come now." Bianca runs her fingers through her luxuriant hair. "A big, bad *sister* like you getting scared by a couple girls like us?"

Half of her tone is condescending, and so is the other half.

"Yeah, who just appears out of the woods like that," I splutter, still trying to make sense of this place, these people, this night, "and doesn't say anything? I called you guys, like, four times. Why didn't you answer?"

Alice makes a face. "It's really loud in there. All those crickets."

"I don't hear any crickets."

They say nothing.

It's like they've all agreed to say nothing.

Or maybe I'm overreacting.

I mean, I *did* just get date groped. Vampire or no, I'm still prone to basic overreaction mode.

What did I really see? And besides, now they are standing right in front of me under the patio lights, happy and smiling. Or at least smiling.

"Nice jacket." Bianca reaches out to touch it. "Why does it look so familiar?"

"That's what I get for shopping at Target," I bluff.

Cara wrinkles her nose. "It's a little big."

"It's way big," Alice says. "Like a-guy-let-you-borrow-it-because-it's-so-cold-out big."

Stupid Alice and her stupid big mouth. She's borrowed, what, four thousand guys' jackets, and I've never said two words. I show up in one—*one*—in all this time and she has to go and make a big deal out of it? In front of *Bianca*, no less?

"Yeah, so this is a coed school, right?" I turn around to put an end to the jacket conversation.

Bianca smiles. "Speaking of boys, aren't you late for a very important date? Something about zombies or werewolves or vampires if I eavesdropped correctly?"

Oh, God, the witch is right!

Zander.

Grover.

Me.

Zombies.

Movie marathon.

Hours ago.

But how would she know? When did she have the chance to eavesdrop on us?

I guess she was right. Nightshade is the kind of place where you know everything about everybody.

"Oh, shoot!" Over my shoulder, I echo Tristan's parting words, "We're not through here."

Is it my imagination when somebody says, "Not by a long shot, Lily"?

CHAPTER 19

I don't knock on Zander's door so much as kick it open.
"Whoa!" Grover sits up in his easy chair, which
would look more at home on the command deck
of the Starship Enterprise, in the process spilling a
double batch of triple butter popcorn on his lap.

"What the?" Zander says from the tiny kitchen
area, where he's pouring tap water into an overflowing
pitcher of Grape-Ade and glaring at me.

"Lily?" Grover scoops a handful of popcorn out
of his lap and shoves the kernels into his mouth.

"Hmm." Zander turns off the faucet, looks at his
weak Grape-Ade, and leans rakishly in the doorway.
"You're right on time for the credits, Lily. Thanks for

showing up so soon."

"I know." I gasp, not quite out of breath but out of patience with myself, with the Sisters, with this whole operation. "I'm sorry. I just had some homework and forgot. I'm so sorry."

Zander spots Tristan's jacket right away. "Hmm, was your assignment to borrow some big guy's jacket and wear it all sexy-like over your shoulders?"

I cock my head, about to apologize, when good old Grover steps in: "He's joking."

A hand reaches up from a fake grave on their big-screen TV.

"Look," Grover says, "another movie's starting right now. You're just in time. She's just in time, Zander," he shouts toward the kitchen, like he's half of a bickering, old married couple. "Don't be rude, dude. Come and join us."

Zander ignores him, ignores me, pours out his light purple drink, and starts all over again. He makes much ado about it, huffing and puffing and tearing and pouring and measuring.

I drift into the dorm suite area. The room is warm and smells vaguely of guys who spend way too much time in front of the TV, eating out of the microwave, and hiding candy bar wrappers under the couch. It's not an entirely unpleasant smell.

Grover is normally polite to a fault, at least to me. But tonight he is glued to some B-rate (maybe even C-rate) zombie flick about a zombie. In a bride dress. Marrying a zombie groom. In a tux.

I notice the *Star Wars* posters again and realize they aren't just framed and evenly spaced. They're in order of release, from *Episode IV*, the first, to *Episode III*, the last. Impressive. Not everybody remembers that.

The spaceship models hanging from the ceiling aren't just good but excellent. I'm talking down-to-the-detail excellent with the right pilots in the right vehicles, with plenty of burn marks and bullet holes to look like they've flown straight out of the silver screen. (Hey, you live forever, you watch a lot of movies. Even *Star Wars*. You should hear me wax poetic on the Terminator series, you *really* want an earful.)

Next to Grover's seat, there's a papasan chair with metal legs, a lime-green cushion, and a matching Yoda throw pillow, which I clutch to my stomach as I sink in.

I can feel Grover's warmth oozing from his massive body in the next seat over. He looks away from his precious screen (that athlete's foot commercial might have something to do with it), sees Zander still mixing his precious Grape-Ade, and says quietly, "Thanks for coming. I know I'm breaking some kind of bro code or whatever by telling you this, but he was really upset when you didn't show earlier."

"I know. I just got carried away."

He looks at the too big leather jacket and says, swishing his finger for maximum effect, "I hope he was worth it, girlfriend."

I slap one of his massive shoulders.

He clutches his popcorn bowl protectively. "Seriously, though, that massive thing is way obvious. Why don't you give it to me and I'll stow it in the closet?"

I do.

By *stow it in the closet*, apparently he means *toss it on the floor amidst a pile of dirty black jeans and one giant Chewbacca slipper*.

He offers me a smaller, separate bowl of popcorn from a small table to his left.

When I decline politely, he smiles and says, "Look, this one never touched my lap, honest."

I'm not convinced.

"Zander made it for you special, Lily. He'll be upset if you don't at least try it."

I sigh and accept it, reaching my hand in and grabbing a few kernels from down in the middle of the bowl, where they're still vaguely warm.

I can't eat much, but I can stick them in my mouth and let them dissolve without much interference in the old vampiric digestive system, if you know what I mean.

Before they're even between my lips, however, I can feel my fingers itching.

By the time the salty corn has reached my tongue, it's already too late.

"Yowzers," I say, greedily wiping my sizzling fingers off on one of Grover's pant legs on the floor. "This is . . . spicy!"

Luckily a zombie attack is happening mid-screen, so Grover can't be bothered. I quickly spit out the offending kernels but it's not enough. My smoking tongue needs instant relief before it gets too damaged.

I panic, looking around, until I find a giant plastic cup sweating just out of Grover's reach. I grab it and pour its contents into my mouth, the dark brown soda and slushy ice cubes working to delay and, eventually, counteract the damaging effects from the popcorn.

"Dang, girl!" Grover says, hand reaching absently

for where his soda cup used to be. "Guzzle much?"

"Sorry." I gasp, grateful to still be able to talk. "What, exactly, did Zander put on that popcorn, Grover?"

He smirks and holds up a saltshaker the size of most oil cans. On its side, in big green letters it says *Garlic Powder.*

"No wonder," I say, fanning my steaming, healing tongue.

"What, you allergic or something?" he asks, eyes still wide.

"Something," I answer, the moment passing, the damage done and, thanks to such a small sprinkling of garlic powder, quickly undone.

Still, that was a close call! Too close, if you ask me.

The movie flickers back to life, and Grover loses all interest in me.

Meanwhile, Zander has moved on to the next course. I hear a pot slam in the kitchen and lean in to Grover. "Maybe I should check on him."

"Gooth idearsh," he mumbles around a mouthful of buttery popcorn, not even bothering to look at me as a hungry zombie groom devours some poor waitress in a backwoods diner. Why are B movies always set in the backwoods? And who would get married there, even if you *were* a zombie bride? And what will they throw at her as she walks down the aisle? Chicken gizzards?

I somehow extricate myself from the papasan chair and walk to the kitchen doorway, fingertips still pink and puckered from my close encounter of the garlic kind.

"Hey." I lean on the doorway between the living room and the kitchen.

"Hey," he grumbles, scraping homemade Chex mix off a cookie sheet and into a large white plastic bowl.

"I'm sorry."

He still hasn't looked at me. "Me too. I'm sorry I went to all this stupid trouble and look like a dope."

"Better a dope than a jerk."

He looks at me, cracks half his crooked smile, and says, "Yeah, I guess you're right, *jerk*."

"Thanks, *dope*!"

He slugs me gently.

I slug him back.

"Do you mind telling me," I ask after an awkward silence, "why you two have an actual kitchen in your dorm room?"

"Oh, this?" Zander smirks, pointing to the small appliances in the broom closet–sized space. "This is a perk for working in the kitchen seven days a week for the last three frickin' years. You want to help us out four hours every day? I can see about getting you an elf-sized microwave too."

"I guess that's fair," I say.

"Fair?" He snorts. "Fair would be a private heli-copter and a trust fund, but we'll take what we can get. Here, help me carry this out to feed the junk food black hole, better known as my roommate."

I grab the bowl, still hot, the scent of buttery, chocolaty pretzels and marshmallows reminding me of slumber parties, pillow fights, eighties records, and bad hair. Of a life long gone; a mortal life, with mortal rules. And actual records—the vinyl kind!

A Target commercial is on, so Grover actually favors us with his presence for a change. "Uhmmm." He trades out his popcorn for Zander's latest cre-ation. "We must have a special guest, Lily, because I'll have you know my man Zander here doesn't make his homemade s'mores Chex mix for any old coed."

I think Zander's blushing, though it's hard to tell in the glowing red glare of the Target commercial.

Instead of the standard-issue couch and end chair and coffee table setup like the one in our suite, Grover and Zander have a kind of man cave setup with the two recliners for themselves (and of course a guest chair just for me).

I'm wondering if that's a perk for working in the kitchen as well or just their prerogative for having stayed in the same dorm room so long.

I huff and grumble my way into my awkward chair.

Zander laughs. "You wanna switch?" he says, already halfway standing.

"Nah," I say, watching the zombie who's been stumbling and grasping to reach his next victim . . . for two full minutes. "The movie actually looks better from down here."

"Hmm," he says, sitting back down and staring at the screen. "Maybe I should try that. It looks pretty bad from up here."

We laugh at Grover's intentness. It's like he's not just watching the movie; he's studying it. Even when Zander throws stale popcorn at him, he only whispers, "Quit it. *Quit* it. Quit *it*," his focus remaining on the movie.

Zander is close, but I wish I could see him better from this angle. He scowls at me and at the screen, alternately, until the scratching at the window starts and we both scowl at that.

"Did you hear that?" Zander looks past Grover

to the shadowy windows.

It's just after midnight. I'm looking for branches, anything that might make a scraping sound like that in the middle of the night.

Grover ignores us when we stand and walk toward the window, the scratches growing louder.

Those aren't branches. I know before I even get to the window.

Those are claws. Specifically, vampire claws. I'd know them anywhere.

What did Tristan say before he stormed off, favoring the finger I'd slapped when he'd gotten fresh? *We're not through here.*

Is he making good on his threat? Here? And how would he know where Zander and Grover's room was? Or that I'd be in it this late on a school night? Did Bianca tell him? The closer we get, the louder the scratching. When we're near enough to look out of their third-floor window, it suddenly stops.

Zander goes for a better look, his face nearly to the glass.

I yank him back. Hard.

I look back to see him standing in the middle of the room next to the coffee table, where his legs have disrupted a stack of Grover's graphic novels.

He's traveled four feet without a sound.

"Lily?" He gasps.

At least he's behind me if anything should happen.

"Are you on some kind of illegal drugs I should know about? Specifically, Olympic-grade steroids?"

"Shhh," I hiss, looking at the window, but the TV is flickering and the only thing I can see is my reflection. I listen intently for more scratching but don't hear any.

Zander, who's crept up, asks behind my shoulder, "What is it?"

"I dunno," I whisper. "Can you get him to turn it down?"

We both look at Grover, who's engrossed in another epic, if creepingly slow, zombie battle.

"Good luck," Zander says.

I tsk but know he's right. "Are there trees outside your window? Bushes?" I ask hopefully.

"No trees, and they'd have to be really tall bushes. We're on the third floor, remember?" His breath spills warm on my neck.

"Sorry, I know that! I'm just . . . wait. Shhh."

Then comes a tapping, rhythmic and constant, seemingly at the top of the tallest window.

Tap.

Tap.

Tap.

Steady, controlled, deliberate.

Like the living room in every dorm suite, Zander's has three windows: a tall one in the middle, two smaller ones on either side. Each has a high, gabled point and a bulky protruding sill for frames or plants or, in the boys' case, a full-scale replica of the planet Tatooine.

The windows are lead framed and seem heavy to open, with those latch locks in the middle.

"Check those," I say, and Zander knows what I mean.

"They're locked. Shoot, they've probably never been opened. We're not exactly the outdoorsy type, you—"

"What's going on?" Grover says, suddenly at our backs.

Hmm, must be a commercial break.

Zander looks mildly irritated, like maybe he thought this was our own private Fright Fest. "Nothing, Grover. Go back to your movie."

But a new one has started. Maybe Grover's already seen it. "This looks like more fun," he says and then, once he's quieted down enough to hear the tapping, "What's that?"

"We don't know," I whisper so he'll hush.

The tapping starts to alternate with scraping.

Tap-tap-tap.

Scrape-scrape.

Tap-tap-tap.

Scrape-scrape.

Yup, it's definitely deliberate.

Grover's eyes are big, and he's suddenly standing next to Zander, so close I keep waiting for them to hold hands.

The TV screen is still flickering behind us, wreaking havoc on our view through the window.

I tell Grover to turn it off.

Amazingly, he does.

There is still light coming from the bathroom, the kitchen, Zander's bedroom. Zander joins Grover, and they race around turning them off one by one. They're in different rooms when they hit the last of the light switches and the suite suddenly blacks out.

With no reflection blocking what's on the other side of the window, the image is crystal clear and absolutely frightening.

I see claws and fangs, both a blur, the scraping and tapping stopped. A figure, too quick to be human and dressed all in black, zips from the top of the center window to the smaller one to my right.

Zander and Grover emerge from their rooms.

"What was that?" Grover says.

The last trace of the shadowy shape vanishes.

I'm panicking, wondering what to say, how to lie, when Zander, still in his doorway, asks, "A bird?"

"Yeah." I turn around, eager to get their attention off the window. "That's what I thought too."

Grover, the true creature feature aficionado, shakes his head. "I dunno, you guys, that was a pretty big bird."

"Lot you know," I say, trying to sound light-hearted. I punch one of his arms and settle nervously into my green chair. "Black birds look bigger at night. Especially when all those zombie movies in a row have you so scared."

That does the trick. Nothing like calling a guy chicken, especially a guy like Grover, to take his mind off the Vamplayer hovering out in the gloom.

"I'm not scared," he says, pressing the remote control dramatically as the TV screen flickers back to life, "but you should prepare to be when *Zombie Mutants 4* wraps you in its spell." He makes one of those evil mastermind "whoo-hooo-haaa-haaa" sounds while rubbing his ham hands together.

Zander and I groan.

The two boys become absorbed in the roving band of zombie mutants (is there any other kind?). I glance at the three gabled windows at the other end of the room, half expecting them to implode at any moment.

They don't, and eventually I relax too, caught up in the spell of the movie or, at least, the boys' enjoyment of it.

But in the back of my mind, I'm thinking of the shape, how big it was, how fast it moved, and wondering, *Was Tristan wearing black when we parted?*

Zander walks me to my room after the last zombie has eaten the last brain in the last frame of the last god-awful living dead flick of the night. He has long forgotten the tap-scratching at his windows. And as he lingers near me, tall, soft, and alive, I tell myself I have as well.

If only that were true.

It's after two in the morning. We shouldn't be out roaming the halls, period, but the night has taken on such a surreal quality—between the blood wine and Tristan's roving hands and Bianca and the girls appearing from the tree line and the scratch-tapping—that it only feels right to be in a gothic walkway hours after curfew. All alone. Shadows dancing beyond the huge stained glass windows. Only our footsteps (hopefully) tapping on the cool marble floors. I mean, the only things missing are a fog machine and fake spiderwebs in the rafters.

Now that we've made up, Zander seems calmer, at peace. He grabs my hand about halfway to my room. It's so warm.

Everyone back at the Academy has such cold hands. It's always a treat to hold a mortal boy's hand.

"So, what do you do for fun around here?"

He laughs. "You mean, besides watch Grover eat popcorn and put together *Star Wars* replicas? You're looking at it."

What a nice life. What a normal, cozy, human life.

I know many girls would run at the sight of the first Yoda throw pillow. Not me. At this point I've had enough charmers, charlatans, slick talkers, and Vamplayers. Give me a tall, strapping, curly-haired, crooked-smiling, pug-nosed, Vader-boxer-shorts-wearing, good guy any day of the week.

I think of how unfair I've been to Zander by meeting with Tristan, leading him on, kissing him. Mission or no mission, it's my job to help humans, not hurt them—not even their feelings.

If only I could go back in time, say no to Tristan, ignore him. I'm supposed to be less susceptible to a Vamplayer's charms, not more.

Maybe the Academy is doing it wrong. Maybe they need a Simulator for deflecting the Vamplayers' emotional seduction, not so much his fighting.

Still, I only have myself to blame. Deep down, I wanted to go with Tristan, wanted to be with him, my own kind, embracing the night, gorging on blood wine and the limitless potential of an evening spent with another immortal. How did I let this creep get to me after all the Vamplayers I've put down over the years?

"Careful," Zander says, extricating his hand from my increasingly tightening grip. "I don't know what you're thinking about, but he must be some kind of a jerk to make you squeeze that hard."

"Sorry."

I have got to talk to Dr. Haskins about my anger reflex. As I age it's getting stronger, not weaker.

"I do that," I explain without explaining.

"Who were you thinking about?" he asks in the weak lamplight bordering the gothic stone walls.

"Nobody special."

"I'm not blind, Lily. I know what Tristan's jacket looks like."

I shake my head and let him speak.

"I don't blame you, okay?" He puts his big hands in front of him. "Let's see." He raises his left hand above his shoulder in a scales-of-justice motion. "You've got the smooth Euro trash player here." Now he brings his other hand way low. "And the geeky dishwasher-slash-busboy-slash-financial-aid guy down here. I get it, okay? I do. I just, I don't blame you."

"Blame me for what?" I ask, but I'm not snappy anymore. I'm more curious.

He blushes and hangs his head, adorably. "Nothing. It's just, Grover warned me about you."

I slug him. "He did, huh? You mean Grover, expert in all things girl?"

"Yeah. If they're zombies maybe. No, he said you were out of my league, that I should watch out or I'd, you know, get my heart broken."

"Out of your league?" Secretly, I'm thanking Grover for at least thinking that much of me. "That's why I was sitting alone at dinner tonight?"

"Not for long." Suddenly his lean body is several inches closer than before.

I flinch at the memory of how charming Tristan was, at least until he turned not so charming. "It's not easy, you know, being the new girl. Everybody's watching, taking notes, comparing, testing you. I thought Cara and Alice had my back. They usually do, but I was vulnerable, okay? It was stupid, and I'm sorry."

"No biggie." He's nonchalant, but I can tell he means it.

"No," I say, touching his chest. "It is a biggie. I had a choice tonight. Hang out with some creep or with some really great guy. Obviously, I made the wrong one. I'm sorry."

He grins, looking down at me, his back up against the wall (when did that happen?). He blinks, those chocolate eyelashes in slow motion, and says, "Now, which one's the creep again? 'Cause I'm confused."

"Shut up."

Before I know it, he's scooped me closer, and his fingers are brushing my cheek, moving a lock of my hair out of the way so he can kiss me.

He is gentle, so gentle.

Even so, the fire rages inside: the ancient, primal, animal fire that ignites whenever my unnatural endorphins flow.

Even now, just swapping spit, he is in danger of swallowing part of me. Part of my eternal me.

And still the blood gurgles deep, bathing me

in warm feelings as his hands slip easily around the small of my back to pull me in, closer, closer, as I lose myself against the rapid thumping of his heart.

He sighs into my throat, feathers my cheek and jawline with soft kisses. It doesn't feel practiced or smooth, like it does with some guys, but exploratory and genuine, like he really wants to take his time and learn what it's like to kiss me.

Little old me.

The Third Sister, finally first in somebody's eyes.

I let him kiss me. I let him explore despite the late hour, the sparse, spooky setting, the former tapping-scratching. I want him to.

I explore as well, tracing his arm from his hand to his shoulder, caressing his neck as he moans softly, eyes closed, and pulls me to his lips once more.

The fire is more intense this time, building in cycles, getting dangerously close.

I can feel the fangs below my gum line quivering now, tingling, eager to dash forth and pluck the life from his jugular. It's automatic; I almost can't help it. My fingernails jut into claws, digging at the waistband of his baggy jeans.

"Yikes." He yanks his head back, smacking the rough-hewn stone wall behind him. "Ouch," he says, laughing, licking a drop of blood off his lip.

"Sorry," I say, eyes downcast out of shame. I give my fangs—my stupid fangs—time to retract. "I get carried away." (Well, that's kind of an understatement.)

"I like that." He tries to sound smooth, though I notice he's not coming back for more. "Just remind me to bring my first-aid kit next time."

"Jerk," I say, slapping his arm as he drags me to my room.

His long legs outpace mine. His warm hands dwarf mine.

His smile is as bright as it was before I bit him.

Too soon we are at the door to my suite. Despite his slightly swollen lower lip, he leans in hesitantly once more.

I kiss him prudishly, with a peck on the lips, nothing more, denying the hunger, the pain, the shame, the bliss, the heat threatening to rise from my toes, through my belly, and into my jaws. Before it's too late, I push him away.

He sighs. "I'm glad you came tonight, Lily." He strolls away.

"Me too." I linger by the door like some lovesick teenager. "I'm glad I picked the good guy."

He cups his hand behind his ear like maybe he

can't hear me so well. "What's that? It sounded like you said you picked the good kisser. I'm glad you think so."

As he walks all the way down the hall, he chuckles.

Oh, wait. That's just me.

CHAPTER 21

Cara and Alice are waiting up for me when I quietly enter the dorm suite, my lips still warm from Zander's kiss, my dead heart still racing, my body all aquiver as the cells remember his warm, gentle touch.

They're in my bedroom, each leaning against one side of the doorjamb and looking in.

I breathe a sweet sigh of relief. They are still my Sisters. They haven't forsaken me after all.

Standing in the middle of the living room suite, I put my hand over my heart, mock gasp, and say, "You guys do love me."

After Zander's butterfly kisses and praying mantis hands, I'm all atwitter. I'm not usually so cheerful. Especially around two chicks who haven't missed an opportunity to diss me all week.

Alice turns around first, almost snapping to attention like I've caught her reading my diary or something. Yeah, like I'd ever keep one of those around with a snoop like Alice for a Sister.

She is followed shortly by Cara, who moves so quickly it looks like it must hurt.

They share another one of those sneaky looks they've perfected recently. "Lily?" they say, as if I'm their mom getting home a day early from vacation. It's not a happy-to-see-me sound.

"Yeah, I'm Lily. Remember me? I live here. Right here, actually."

I walk toward my room, tired after the long night, exhausted really. They move closer together so I can barely see through their sleek, muscular shoulders. I imagine it's a move they train the president's body-guards in. You know, the Filling the Door tactic or something wicked cool like that. It's like they squeeze out all the light in the room. Even their heads inch toward one another's, making them seem impenetrable.

What, are they taking night classes at the Academy or something? I'll have to look into those when we get back.

The already surreal night has taken on cartoon-ish dimensions.

"What gives, you guys?" I chuckle.

I try to budge through them and fail. "I need to change and get some sleep. Come on, scram."

"Well—" Alice begins hesitantly, avoiding my eyes.

Cara cuts her off. "We thought you'd be bunking with the boys tonight." Her voice is a little firm, a lot decisive, and almost defensive.

"What? I'm not shacking up with some guy I just met," I say good-naturedly, as if we're in our own dorm back at the Academy, playing the fools after another Stake Training class. "You must have me confused with Alice or something."

Not a laugh, not a chortle, not a guffaw. I practically hear crickets chirping in the audience.

Out of nowhere, their words begin tripping and whirring into one unbelievable development that, in a million years, I'd never see coming.

"Well, Bianca was so upset when she saw you wearing Tristan's jacket earlier tonight and—"

"Where is Tristan's jacket, by the way?"

"We kind of invited her to stay over."

"Did he come back and get it? Because, I mean, you had it earlier."

"And we felt so bad for the girl—"

"It looked expensive. I hope you didn't lose it."

"That we kind of gave her your room—"

"And she's kind of in there—"

"Right now!"

Oh.

No.

They.

Didn't.

I shove them aside.

They're not bluffing. This is not a joke.

Bianca Ridley isn't just in my dorm suite in the middle of the night. She's not just in my *room* at two in the morning.

Bianca.

Ridley.

Is.

In.

My.

Frickin'.

Bed!

Touching my sheets.

Fluffing my pillows.

Invading my most personal of personal spaces.

"Are you guys out of your flipping *minds*?"

They don't answer, don't even flinch.

"You've got to be joking. Seriously? Guys? Can someone explain to me why Bianca Ridley is in my bed wearing my favorite nightgown?"

"We just did," Alice says, as if their incoherent rambling about Bianca and Tristan and the almighty jacket could possibly explain, let alone excuse, the social indignity of these proportions.

"I didn't want it." Bianca sits up against my fluffy white pillows. All three of them. Even the sham I use just for show! She picks at one of the spaghetti straps on my favorite nightgown, the black one, the one that hugs my curves and drapes to the floor and scoops at the neck and doesn't bunch up at my waist. The one I was hoping to wear, you know, when I was finally First Sister and invited to seduce the Vamplayer one of these days.

It's defiled, wrecked, ruined.

What, they couldn't have given her the ratty old XL T-shirt I sleep in when I haven't done my laundry for a few days?

"I told them it was too big, Lily, but you know these two. So generous. They wouldn't let me say no."

"Oh, they're generous, all right." I grab my robe off the door and pick up a throw pillow Bianca obviously tossed on the floor. "And if my hands weren't full, I'd give them something too."

I huff past my Sisters and flop on the couch, burrowing my face deep in the cushions to choke back the tears. I grab the purely decorative throw as my blanket against the chill October air seeping through the windowsills.

I hear muffled conversation behind me, and it takes every ounce of my considerable willpower to not turn around and stare daggers at my room or launch an errant pillow at the girls' heads.

Two sets of footsteps move along my bedroom floor, the pitter-pattering kind you hear on Christmas morning. Several sets of cheek kisses. (What? Those witches never kissed *me* to sleep before.) The door shuts.

Cara and Alice stomp to my side. No pittering and pattering or cheek kisses for me.

"What is *wrong* with you?" Alice hisses inches away from my face.

"I can't believe how rude you were just now," Cara says.

"Me? Rude?" I turn around to face them, hardly believing what I'm hearing. "What about you guys? Bianca? In my bed? I've heard of switch-hitting before, but don't you guys think you're taking it to the next level with this chick?"

I'm whispering so low they can barely hear, but of course we can hear a fly buzz at the window, so it's no great feat for them to lean closer and continue telling me how wrong, stupid, and pig-headed I am, have been, and probably always will be.

"Hey," Alice says, "we're doing what we're supposed to, remember? This is our job. Your job too if you weren't so busy hanging around with your fan boys."

"How can I join you when half the time I don't even know where you are?"

Cara shakes her head. "You know how it gets on assignment. This isn't your first time at the rodeo. An opportunity presents itself, you take it."

"Fine, yeah, I get that, but would a heads-up be too much to ask? Like tonight. I sat there like a fool all dinner wondering where you two were."

They stand there, tapping their feet, ignoring my question.

"And what was with that crap out in the woods earlier?"

"What crap?"

"What woods?"

"Don't play me. Out by the picnic area when

you were with Bianca."

They smile at each other, frown at me.

"We were just playing," Cara says.

Alice looks right at me. "Yeah, can't you even take a joke anymore?"

"It didn't look like a joke, you two. It looked creepy is what it looked like. And what about the whole spitballs-in-the-hair incident?"

They lean together, check to see if my bedroom door is closed. It is.

Alice says, "That was Bianca's idea."

"No duh. So why did you join her?"

"We had to," Cara says. "How would it look if we didn't?"

"I dunno, like maybe *you were my Sisters*?"

They share another side eye.

"And quit doing that."

"Doing what?" they ask oh-so-innocently.

"Giving each other the googly eyes all the time. We're Sisters, dammit! You include me. I asked you a question. Where were you tonight?"

They avoid the side eye, although I know it's tempting.

"Bianca asked us into town," Cara says. "We figured it would be a good idea to accept. Wouldn't you have done the same?"

"Okay, yeah, but isn't the goal to get all three of us accepted into her fold? How is she supposed to warm up to me when you guys keep shutting me down?"

"Hey," Alice says, "it's not our fault you took a detour to a galaxy far, far away our first day here. How were we supposed to explain *that*?"

"All right, I get it, but we need to regroup, get our heads in the game. You're right. You're doing what you're supposed to, but I'm sorry. I feel left out."

There is another awkward silence.

I shake my head. "Has she at least said anything about Tristan yet? I know you're having fun with your new girlfriend and all, but you do remember Tristan, don't you? Our potential Vamplayer?"

They share another look. I let it go this time.

"Bianca's being coy," Cara says, "but give us a few days and she'll spill."

"Forget her," Alice says. "What about you? Why were you in Tristan's jacket tonight anyway? Looks like we're not the only ones keeping secrets."

"Well, if either of you had bothered to speak to me when you were playing hide-and-go-creep in the forest, I could have told you that, yes, he asked me to dinner and, yes, he is definitely

Prime Suspect Number One on my Probably Is a Vamplayer list."

They look a little skeptical.

Alice says, "Like why?"

Now they look a lot skeptical.

"Like, he can keep up with me when we run on the track in the morning. Like—"

"Whoa, whoa, back up, girl," Cara says, some of the old lifeblood running through her veins. "What track? What run?"

I tell her, and she smiles, looking vaguely impressed.

"Go on," Alice says, looking unimpressed. (Remind me: why is she First Sister again?)

"At dinner tonight, he only ate stuff with blood in it."

That perks them up.

"Like what?" Cara says.

I tell them.

"What, you mean not out of bags or anything?" Alice says.

"Dude, how many high school juniors do you know who consider blood sausage a delicacy?"

"Yeah," Cara says, "but you know these prep school dudes. They're different that way."

This is going to be harder than I thought. "Well,

he has this oddly, I dunno, European accent. What about that?"

"Like Transylvanian European?" Alice says, suddenly interested.

"I can't tell exactly, but he's definitely not from Alabama, if you know what I mean."

They wait expectantly for more, but I realize that's all I've got. Fast running, a fondness for blood sausage, and talking like a character from a bad (Transylvanian) soap opera.

"Hmm," Alice says, "it's hardly enough to send Dr. Haskins for approval to act."

"I know, but at least it's something. What do you guys have?"

No answer. Not a thing.

I yawn, patting my stiff brocade pillow and preparing for a long, uncomfortable night. "Well, okay then, maybe in between skinny-dipping and trips to town, you could come up with a little thing we at the Academy like to call evidence."

Cara snaps impatiently, as if she's on Team Alice for once, "Well, you're going to have to trust us on this one."

"Yeah, there's a reason you're still Third Sister, 'kay? Dr. Haskins trusts us over you because we actually know what we're doing."

I shake my head, still concerned but so tired.

Without another word, Alice yawns and pads across the hardwood floor to her bedroom and shuts the door.

"Am I overreacting?" I ask Cara, desperate for answers, feeling unplugged, unglued, and out of whack.

She shrugs. "A little, but you're right. We need to regroup. Give us a few days to get Bianca all the way over on Team Sisters, and then we'll tell her the truth. Until then, ignore what you see, okay?"

"Why?" I ask of her forehead as she avoids my eyes. I wish she'd look at me for once. "What am I going to see?"

"Well, you know how girls get when they take sides. It could get ugly tomorrow and the next few days, so just don't take it personal."

"What does that mean?"

But she's already walking away.

Could get ugly?

Uglier than standing me up for dinner tonight?

Uglier than spooking me out in the woods?

Uglier than giving Bianca my frickin' bed?

Uglier than firing spitballs at my back?

If that's not ugly, what does tomorrow bring?

CHAPTER 22

I get my answer at sunrise. It's not pretty.

In fact, the whole next day is a scene straight out of *Heathers*.

The unrated version.

For vampires.

I wake up late, sore, crooked, my throw blanket on the floor, feet freezing, pillow behind my back, facedown in this hundred-year-old (probably) bed-bug-infested (likely) couch.

The girls giggle in the bathroom.

I've woken up in an episode of *The Twilight Zone* called "Opposite Day at the Crazy Dorm for Back-Assward Giggly Girls Who Steal Your Bed at Night and Wear Your Makeup the Next Morning."

It's like all of a sudden those three are the Sisters and I'm the bad guy.

I unfold my bent body off the couch and slink over toward them, a stranger in my own dorm room.

I clear my throat, indicating I'd like to use the bathroom at some point, and they look at each other, roll their eyes at me—*roll their eyes at me*—and go back to giggling and mascara swapping.

I blow my hair out of my face, stomp into my room, notice Bianca hasn't even had the decency to make my bed, gather my backup makeup kit, some panties, a bra, and some ridiculous outfit, and then stomp out of the suite and all the way to the bathroom down the hall. (Gross.)

Believe it or not, the day only gets worse from there.

Nightshade is all abuzz about this new allegiance. It's like a red carpet opening for some *Sex and the City* remake, high school edition.

For one, the trio seem to have acquired a whole new wardrobe, like, overnight.

Is that what they *really* went to town for?

Bianca is in an emerald dress, no bra—and, man, are these halls frigid. The vague outline of some daring porn star panties press against the silky green material, and a slim raven belt is wound twice around her hourglass waist. Her emerald heels clatter so loudly through the marble-tiled halls they must have taps.

Cara is in a snug white jumpsuit with all black accessories: heels, belt, scarf, shades. Her corn-rows are gone, and she's somehow had her hair straightened. It looks fab, but it's odd to see this honor student pulling off the sleazy-weazy look.

Alice, of course, is working the *Lady in Red* look: suede pants, platform pumps, lambskin jacket, big sunglasses.

It's like they're in some all-girl band and they've chosen their colors.

The rock star comparison doesn't end there.

I only have one class with them (which is starting to feel like one too many), but in the halls—er, their own personal catwalk—I practically hear paparazzi cameras capturing their every long-legged, high-heeled, hip-swishing step.

They walk arm in arm everywhere. To the bathroom, to the water fountain, to their lockers.

Bianca is in the middle, natch, Cara on the left, Alice on the right.

I watch, like the rest of the school, transfixed by their beauty, their perfection, their sudden popularity.

We're only juniors, but it's like overnight my Sisters have joined Bianca at the top of the popularity heap.

Even senior girls stand by, nearly bowing as the new Sisters slink past.

They look at no one, answer no one, talk to no one, least of all me. They simply walk into and out of classes, turning heads, making waves while kids part for them like the Red Sea.

I feel bad for the pretty young things Bianca used to hang with before Alice and Cara moved in on their territory. (Not that they feel bad for me, of course.) You can see them in the halls, standing off to the side, leaning forward on their hooker heels when Bianca and her new friends breeze by, their expressions expectant, their hands waving out *remember me?* gestures. Then comes the depression—I'm talking bereavement—when Bianca surges by without so much as a wave.

I normally don't give much thought to what happens to the other humans when we swoop into a school and do our thing, but pain is writ large on these girls' faces. I gotta say, for the record, Cara and Alice suck.

By the time we get to PE I'm prepared for anything, except what actually happens.

I've been kind of dreading the whole locker room smack down moment I've been expecting all day, but luckily that's out of the picture. What actually happens is way worse, but at least it's not in a locker room. There's that, you know?

A note on the door says, "No uniforms today. Meet in gym."

I bypass the locker room and saunter into the gym, looking forward to seeing Zander for the first time all day.

Unfortunately, Tristan has him in a headlock, and Bianca's poking Grover in the chest with her long, solid nails. (Or claws? It's hard to tell from across the gym.)

I don't see Coach Wannamaker, a sub, a dean, or any adult for that matter, but we've still got a few minutes before class starts.

Zander's face is red and blustery, like he's not getting enough air.

Protocol says I'm allowed to reveal myself to save a human life and *only* to save a human life, and I'm thinking this might be the day.

A dozen or so other kids are scattered around the cretins, either cheering or cringing depending which color of ball they got during Vampire Smack

Down Dodgeball Armageddon the other day.

Ignoring them, I stomp to Tristan and yank his hand off Zander's neck in one swift, powerful motion.

He looks vaguely ticked off until he sees it's me who's spoiling all his fun. Then he looks really PO'ed.

"What is your problem?" I shout, but his grip is firm and it's all I can do to wrangle Zander away.

"Ask your boyfriend." Tristan shoves him.

We both go tripping backward, our shoes squeaking on the gym floor. Zander looks more flustered than I feel as he yanks his hand from me and looks away.

Only now do I see the leather jacket pooled at Tristan's ginormous feet.

Zander is gasping next to me, red-faced, looking ticked off, but he'll live.

That's all that really matters at this point: who lives; who dies.

I shove him behind me into a row of bleachers, where he sits unceremoniously on his rump.

A few classmates rush to console him.

"I'm asking *you*, Tristan." I march forward until only a few feet separate us. I have to look up to threaten him.

He doesn't back down. His chest is puffed out

in a stiff white shirt, buttoned only halfway up, the wide collar popped, a light blue T-shirt like a second skin against his firm pecs and flat stomach. He looks radiant, like he's just stepped out of the ocean, his long hair slicked back, his dark eyes fiery. He crosses his arms across that great expanse of chest. "It's refreshing to see a young woman defending her man, rather than the other way around. That's what I love about this country. The men aren't afraid to be humiliated."

"Cut the crap, Tristan, and tell me what happened."

I hear a wheeze and a grunt and see Bianca giving Grover the world's longest, most excruciating-looking titty twister. His face is bright red, his forehead riddled with dewy drops of perspiration, his chin quivering as if at any moment he might let forth the waterworks.

I glare at Alice and Cara to try to guilt them into helping him out, but they ignore me, carefully eying Tristan instead.

"Nothing happened. Nothing that should matter to you anyway. It's between gentlemen, of course. And gentlemen never fight and tell."

"Zander was trying to give his stupid jacket back," Grover says over his pain.

Bianca tires of toying with him and shoves him forward, straight past me and into the bleachers, where Zander is licking his wounds.

"This is all over your stupid jacket?" I kick it across the floor, hearing its zipper clatter under bleachers, where it lands in a crumpled, twisted mess. (Good.)

"Of course not," Tristan sneers.

Bianca rushes to massage his shoulder. In her heels, she's nearly his height. Their heads bow together, the happy couple.

Grover and Zander remain on the sidelines. Alice and Cara stay out of the fray altogether.

Watching Tristan and Bianca coo, I remember his hand under my blouse. "That's fine, Tristan, since we're both being so honest all of a sudden. But why should you have all the fun? Why don't I tell Bianca what happened after you gave me the—"

The slap hits me from out of the blue, so fast, so hard it could only have come from a vampire's hand.

I hear a response ripple through the gym, though with my ears ringing it's hard to tell who's gasping and who's jeering. I look, my eyes stinging, to find Bianca standing in front of Tristan, holding him back from hitting me again, one of her hands pressed firmly on his chest.

He stands behind her, glowering, and I shake my head.

I can feel my claws growing, a natural pain response as my immortal body fights years of fight-or-flight adaptation. I shove my fists in my pockets, fighting my vampire urges to get control of my mortal, teenage self. It's not working. And it's not just the claws. I feel the swell of fangs beneath my gums and keep my mouth closed.

Cara and Alice walk toward me, their heels clicking on the gym floor. For only a fraction of a second, I think they'll finally come to my aid and offer at least a word of comfort, even if it's on the down low while Bianca is tending to Tristan.

Instead, they stand next to Bianca and link arms.

Tristan still lurks in the background out of frame. The "Sisters" won't even let him between them.

I frown, glad I can no longer cry.

Paper crinkles somewhere in the distance, and a quiet voice says, "Class? Yes, please, class? Over here, thank you. My name is Mr. Sanford, and I'll be your sub for this period."

A diminutive man stands in the middle of the gym floor, a folded newspaper under one armpit, a briefcase dangling from one hand. He drones on, something about Coach Wannamaker this and appendicitis that.

We cluster in the bleachers for free time, and the sub takes a seat with his back to us, puts the briefcase on his lap, and begins noodling over a crossword puzzle.

My Sisters plus Bianca huddle around Tristan like a harem to their sheik, scowling at me.

I join Zander and Grover way up in the nosebleed section. Hanging our heads, we can hear them laughing, joking down near the gym floor where they sit, a tight cluster of Vamplayer, Sisters, and Bianca nuzzling each other like a pack of monkeys picking nits off each other's hides.

"I'm so sorry," I say to Zander, touching his raw, bruised neck. "I never meant for this to happen."

"You didn't have to defend me."

"Yeah," Grover says, smiling, one bench lower, still rubbing the sting out of one massive moob. "Any minute there, Zander was going to pull one of his Jedi mind tricks and fool Tristan into letting him go."

I laugh and tousle Grover's hair.

"Anyway," Zander says, craning the kinks out of

his neck, "I'm just sorry the chick jack-slapped you like that. She's lucky she's a girl, or I would've been all up in her grill."

"I think the air must not be back in your brain yet. It was Tristan who slapped me, but don't worry. I wouldn't expect you to go up against a guy like him. That dude's bad to the bone."

Grover and Zander share a look.

"She must have really clocked you harder than I thought," Grover says.

"Yeah." Zander touches my shoulder before letting his hand drop. "It wasn't Tristan who slapped you. It was Bianca."

CHAPTER 23

I catch the girls in the locker room, spin Bianca around, and slap her face. It barely moves.

"You witch!" She grabs for my arms, but of course I'm too quick for her (if only barely).

I leap over her and land on the other side, shoving her forward. Her pretty little face slams into the nearest row of lockers. She spins quickly, not bleeding (damn), and advances on me.

Other girls, mortal girls, from class have started to filter in. I can't go full Sister on her, but it doesn't stop me from grabbing her by the neck and jamming her into the lockers again.

She yelps and resists, a fire in her eyes like she'd

kill me if she could. No, like she'd tear me to pieces *then* kill me.

I feel strong hands, familiar hands, on my back. I knock them off, like a Third Sister should. My hand clutches Bianca's neck, not pressing so much as holding.

Alice barks, "Lily, enough. Too many eyes, too many eyes."

I ignore her. They started all this.

Cara says, "Now is not the time or the place."

I ignore her too. She's wrong. For once, the level-headed one, the Second Sister, is wrong. Dead wrong.

Bianca laughs, somehow managing to toss her hair even though I have most of her central nervous system in the palm of my quaking, ready-to-snap-an-epiglottis hand.

"Listen to your Sisters," she says, using the word again like she knows what we are, why we're here, why we're together, why I'm so mad. Like she knew the minute we got here. Like she knew the first day when I was watching her from Headmistress Holly's window.

There is a rumbling at our backs and then the voice of the timid sub. He sticks his hand in the doorway but not his head. "Girls, everything all right? I wouldn't want to have to mention this to

Headmistress Holly."

Mortal girls scatter. Alice and Cara rush to assuage him. The last thing they need is to involve the headmistress. Or any adult, for that matter.

It's just Bianca and I left to our own devices at last.

I loosen my grip on her jugular.

Seizing her opportunity, Bianca grabs my thumb and turns me around. I'm on my knees in three seconds flat, my arm pinned behind me. Back and forth, up and down, she plays my thumb like a joystick. I can nearly hear the bones of my wrist scrape together, the tendons stretch, the muscles sprain.

I grunt. I want to scream but won't give a mere mortal the satisfaction.

She bends me forward and down, down, down, the tension in my arm so tight she could snap it in an instant.

Not that I wouldn't mend, but it would take a while. I'd be on the sidelines for a few days, and I don't have a few days. Not this time, not with this assignment and the way it's gone so screwy so fast.

"Careful." Her mouth is at my ear.

By now my face is dangerously close to the putrid locker room floor. (Hey, even a Vampress has her limits.)

"Your Sisters aren't around to save you. And if I have my way, they won't be your Sisters much longer."

The pain in my arm is excruciating, the pressure on my thumb inhuman, and my nose is practically touching the tiles.

Scrambling feet and sliding sneakers signal my rescue.

She drops me, and only my immortal strength can save me from crumpling on the floor. I stand to face her, but already Cara and Alice are whisking her away.

I rub my shoulder. The rest of the girls flit past, none bothering to stop and see how I am or what happened. What did happen? Because something did. Something wrong, unnatural, almost impossible.

Because while Bianca was trying to make me kiss the tiles, I wasn't just resisting. I was fighting. Hard. With every moment of training, every ounce of energy, every drop of vampire blood, I was struggling to face her, to grab, kick, fight, or bite her—whatever it took.

She never budged, wasn't even winded.

No mere mortal could have held me that way.

Not a bodyguard, soldier, bodybuilder, weight lifter, assassin, marine, or green beret. And definitely not a petite high school junior in emerald heels.

I limp out of the locker room.

Has Tristan already turned her?

And if so, why wouldn't Alice and Cara know by now?

And if they know, why wouldn't they tell me?

Z ander tries to cheer me up after my very long, very horrible, very bad day.

Zander does this by asking me to shoot hoops with him after his dinner shift.

Zander doesn't understand I have a history with basketball.

I don't like it. It doesn't like me back.

Still he's sweet to offer, and even Grover is game when he sees how bummed I am after the whole headlock, titty twister, witch slap incident.

We don't play in the gym, of course. Not only is it strictly off limits after dusk, but there are too many bad memories in there. For all of us. Especially these two.

Instead Zander shows me to a dimly lit but perfectly functional half court behind the cafeteria, where the cooks spend time between the lunch and dinner shifts shooting hoops, smoking butts, and generally gossiping about the students at Nightshade. Or, I suppose, their teachers. Or, in a pinch, pretty little Headmistress Holly.

Grover, who insists he's going to join our game as soon as he finishes stretching, sits on the bench on the outdoor lighted court lazily lifting one arm over his head. "You know, I never thought of Nightshade as a particularly dangerous place before you showed up, Lily."

I mock gasp, holding my hand against my T-shirted chest.

Careful, Lily. He could be onto something here.

"This is all my fault, you guys?" I say.

Meanwhile, Zander sinks another shot, making it ten to zero. Or is it zero to ten? Either way, in case you haven't guessed, not only do I *not* know how to score basketball, but I'm the one with zero.

"Well"—Zander laughs, dribbling the ball in circles around me as he goes up for an easy layup— "strange things *did* start happening when you got here."

Zander passes me the ball. I catch it. With my

stomach. "Like what?" I blurt.

Yes, in case you're keeping score, I could be the most uncoordinated vampire on the planet, maybe in the entire universe.

"Hmm, let's see." From the sidelines, Grover takes yet another sip of his extra large Gatorade, although he's yet to move a muscle (other than to pick up said sport drink, that is). "First you force us into dousing you with water when we meet. Then you alienate us by making us hang out with you. Then—"

"Hold up." I can't help but chuckle. "Alienate you? Unless my memory fails, you guys weren't exactly going to be voted most popular before I showed up."

"Maybe not," Grover concedes, "but you didn't help matters much. Then your girlfriends give us the evil eye all day. Then I almost get my left breast yanked free of my body during gym class. Then poor Zander almost gets his head torn off by that Tristan guy. Then the new girl slaps you. I mean—"

"I thought I was the new girl." I pout and miss another shot.

Zander runs off to retrieve the ball from behind the Dumpster.

Grover shakes his head. "Yeah, well, you're new

too, but before you three Witches of Nightshade showed up, Bianca was the Head Witch in Charge around here."

I shake my head. I hear Zander dribbling the ball in the background. "Wait, hold up. I thought Bianca had been here forever."

He cocks his head and puts down his sports drink. "Uh, I think I'd remember being terrorized by an uberwitch like Bianca for the last three years, thank you very much."

"Yeah," Zander says, all pretense at playing an actual game of hoops dropped as he attempts to spin the ball on one of his long, if crooked, fingers. "She only showed up, what, a week or so before you did."

I think of Tristan, dazzling me with his picnic the night before. "No, you guys. It's Tristan who's the newbie, not Bianca." But even as I say it, the words ring hollow, like the sound of blood not racing through my ears.

Grover rolls his eyes. "I'm sorry, newbie. You're wrong. Tristan transferred here from, like, Pennsylvania two years ago."

"You mean Transylvania," I say.

Were these guys delusional? There's no way a suave, debonair, vaguely European, blood wine–

drinking stud like Tristan could hail from anywhere as white bread as Pennsylvania, of all places.

"Is that what he told you?" Zander says as if I'm the most clueless chick on the planet.

Who knows? Maybe he has a point.

"Man, that's a new one. No, he's suburban as they come. But don't feel bad. Smarter girls have fallen for his Euro-trash shtick."

"What?" I gasp, truly horrified.

"Let me guess," Grover says, and now it's a game for him—for both of them. "The reason you couldn't hang with us for the first feature of our all-night Zombie Fest was that Tristan 'Pennsylvania' Winters asked you for a picnic. Am I right?"

Oh, God.

"With his picnic basket, I bet," Zander says, the ball spinning crookedly on his finger.

No.

"Full of all kinds of imported meats and cheeses."

It can't be.

"What is it, Grover? Blood sausage and head cheese?"

It just can't be.

"Blood cheese," Grover corrects, wagging a finger at him. "That's even grosser than head cheese."

"No, it's not!"

"Yes, Lily, it is. Please. And then, what, blood wine to seal the deal?" Zander says knowingly.

"How? What? How do you guys know all this?"

Zander lets the ball drop to the court, fiddling with it under his feet as he strikes a soccer stance. "We work in the kitchen, remember? Who do you think orders that crap for him?"

"Yeah," Grover says, "those flat-screen TVs and limited edition X-wing models don't come cheap, you know."

"I-I-I don't understand."

"It's simple," Zander explains, sitting on the basketball, his long legs stretched out and crossed at the ankles. He looks up at me, half bemused, half superior. "Tristan can't order the stuff and have it shipped directly to his room. It's considered contraband. If Headmistress Holly finds out, well, she could have him shipped home to Pennsylvania. He has us order it through the kitchen, even pays us up front. When it comes, we stow it in the walk-in cooler and let him know about it. When he shows up to retrieve it, he pays us fifty dollars each for our troubles. Girl, he's been running that scam since sophomore year."

Grover shakes his head.

Zander stands, the ball shooting out from under him, rolling into the murk.

Both boys ignore it.

Game over, I suppose, in more ways than one.

"We expected more from you," Grover says. "You being a woman of excellent taste and all."

Zander nods, long arms crossed.

"Taste?" says a voice from the darkness. Bianca steps from the shadows, clutching Zander's basketball between two pale hands.

She tosses it at him so hard it takes everything he has to catch it, making a sickening thwack.

I catch him shaking his hands loose to lessen the pain.

"This girl has about as much taste as that basketball," she says.

From either side of her, Cara and Alice step out from the shadows, cackling like robots: Bianca's personal version of canned laughter.

"Hey," Grover says, rousing himself to stand and join us at the fringes of the tiny basketball court, "where'd you guys come from?"

No one responds.

I don't think he expected an answer.

Panic grips me as I consider the situation. In an

almost perfect triangulation, the girls have managed to trap us without my even realizing they were doing it.

Cara blocks the woods. We can't escape that way.

Alice blocks the only door into the school. We can't run there.

Bianca paces around the perimeter of the basketball court, hissing like a banshee, baring her eight-inch fangs.

"W-w-what are those?" Grover clings to Zander.

"L-l-lily," Zander sputters. "It's still too early for Halloween. Tell your girl to lose her costume before she freaks someone out."

"Too late." Grover's voice quivers.

The girls patrol their appointed posts, pacing like tigers in their invisible cages.

"I'll explain later," I say to the boys, whose arms cluster around my neck like pearl necklaces. "Whatever I do, just follow me. Zander, hand me the ball."

He does, his hands trembling.

The ball is big and fat in my fingers. "Speaking of taste," I say, aiming, "choke on this." I launch it with every fiber of my vampire being. It sails through the dark with sickening speed. For once, it lands true, lodging in Bianca's extra-long, extra-dangling fangs, where it sticks, like a double shot of taffy, leaving her looking like a sad, deflating jack-o'-lantern as she tries to shake it loose.

I know it won't last long.

Cara and Alice approach, cutting our time even shorter.

I see the light shining in my fourth-story room and shout, "Climb!"

CHAPTER 25

The wall is made of rough-hewn stone, with plenty of jutting crags and hidden handholds. The boys struggle with each foothold like it's their first, legs shaking, feet slipping above me, pushing pebble dust and shoelaces into my eyes.

Both legs firmly planted, I try to hoist Grover's warm, double-wide rear up to the next handhold. "Reach, Grover. You have to help me! This is serious."

"I know this is serious," he shouts.

Eight feet below me the girls circle, smiling like feral cats watching mice scamper out of a drainpipe.

"This is seriously hard for a man my size."

"Okay, well, if these girls grab you, you're going

to be about half your size without even trying."

"How could they do that?" Zander is nearly to the second-floor landing. "They're way down—"

Now, just as I've been expecting this whole time, Alice and Cara float up until their momentum runs out and they cling effortlessly to the stone wall.

"Uh, Lily, why can your girlfriends fly?"

"They're not flying." I grunt, literally shoving Grover onto the second-floor landing.

Grover wheezes, back against the wall, belly trembling. He leans over as far as the thin ledge will allow, gasping for breath.

Zander climbs for the third. He's getting the hang of this, a natural with his long arms and legs, muscles hard and limber from years spent washing dishes and carting bus trays and peeling endless, towering boxes of lettuce.

Inside a random window in our path, a young couple shed clothes like snakes shed their skin, oblivious of us.

"Not flying? Uh, could have fooled me." Zander nearly loses his footing.

I hiss at Cara and Alice, but I'm no match for their double-long fangs and wicked-dense claws.

They linger at the periphery, slashing at Grover's

shirt but not touching his skin, tugging on Zander's shoes but only halfheartedly. It's like they're toying with us, making a game of this.

Zander continues to climb even as Alice reaches ever so playfully for his T-shirt, his soft human skin.

Grover whimpers as Cara's claws slice like butter through a back belt loop.

At least she manages the impossible, urging him to the next foothold without my help.

The sound of breathing is heavy, the scent of human fear and perspiration filling the air like a heady, not unpleasant perfume.

I snatch at Cara's feet, but she scrambles out of reach, hissing at me with those lethal-looking fangs, her face a stranger's, a mask of animal, vampiric, immortal rage.

Alice swoops to defend her.

I swat at her long, graceful thighs, almost losing my balance. I cling to the wall with only my feet for leverage.

My Sisters dangle, laughing, hissing, enjoying this, one keeping me occupied while the other harasses Grover or Zander or both.

We're almost there: the third floor behind us, the fourth out of reach.

What are they waiting for?

They could slice us to bits anytime they choose. So why aren't they?

Alice and Cara hover, harassing the boys, but where is their ringleader, the Head Witch in Charge?

I look down, but she is no longer standing on the ground.

I look left. Not there.

I look right. Not there either.

I sense a presence and turn just in time to see Bianca floating behind me.

"Climb!" I urge, voice hoarse with panic. I'm eager to get to the relative safety of my room as quickly as possible. (Yeah, like glass and walls and doors will stop them.)

Bianca is near but not near, there but not there. Like the other two, she toys with me, hissing in my ear, moving out of range when I swat at her. Flitting into view, then out of range, like a giant hummingbird.

With fangs.

And claws.

On crack.

Grover's sweat drips onto my forehead, and I groan, shoving him up to the next foothold, then one more.

My own fangs are out now, my claws scraping

against his sneakers, slicing the double cuffs of his (very) relaxed fit jeans. If he's surprised by my strength, he doesn't let on. He simply scrambles, whimpering, as I heft him up, up, higher and higher.

Lucky me, all the effort has loosened his already generous jeans to the point that not only can I see the pattern of his size XXL Green Lantern boxer shorts, but the plumber's crack they're supposed to be hiding!

None the wiser, Zander is nearly to the fourth floor.

Seeing him, Alice races to block the window to our room.

I climb to my right.

Cara tousles Grover's hair.

I leap from the wall, pushing Alice into the air along with me.

She hisses violently, an animal noise, retaliating with a swift swipe of her claws at my ankle. Luckily I chose to wear high-tops to tonight's basketball game. The canvas and rubber soles tear, but I don't feel a claw on skin or bone.

She draws back for another swipe.

Zander yanks open the window and dives inside my suite.

Alice is close, ready to leap through, when I kick

her out into the night, reach down, and literally pull Grover into the air. He dangles momentarily, like a wrecking ball swaying on the end of a crane.

Cara grabs his large ankles in a human tug-of-war.

"Release him." Bianca's voice is fierce.

Cara immediately does.

I use the momentum to toss Grover through the window.

He lands with a groan, slamming into the out-dated couch and moving it halfway across the room on its rusty claw feet.

I stand on the landing, guarding the window, ready to do battle until the end, but they just cling to the wall, smiling, laughing.

"What do you want?" I snap, one leg now inside my room, the other on the landing just in case.

"Just to be left alone." Bianca crosses her arms, her long, curved fangs dangling past her chin, saber-toothed tiger–style.

And she hovers and hovers and hovers some more.

But . . . that's impossible.

Only one type of vampire can hover that long: a Royal.

Only one type of vampire has fangs that long: a Royal.

Born, not made, a descendent of the Originals.

But it can't be.

Unless . . . unless Tristan is a Royal and when he turned Bianca, she got the lion's share of his Royal powers.

And where is he anyway?

Why is he letting the girls do all the dirty work for him?

Usually a Vamplayer is more protective of the first girl he turns and rushes in like crazy to defend her if and when we show up.

But now Tristan's MIA.

"Thanks for all your help," I hiss to Cara and Alice, who barely acknowledge me.

"Do what she says," Cara warns, not a trace of concern in her voice. "It's for the best."

"For whom?" I ask, although I already know.

Alice answers, "For us."

"*We* used to be us," I say.

Alice shakes her head. "Not anymore. Now *we're* us, and you're just like *them*." She points to Zander and Grover huddling in the center of our dorm suite, drenched in sweat, the bottom of Zander's T-shirt splattered with tiny drops of blood, Grover tugging at the torn belt loops of his already saggy jeans.

I climb into the room. Both feet on the hardwood floor, both hands on the bottom of the window. "Now what?" I ask, trying not to sound helpless as my mind reels.

"Don't wait up," Bianca says and floats to the ground, Cara and Alice scampering down the walls to join her.

CHAPTER 26

I slam the window shut and lock it tight.

Grover gets the hint and slams the window nearest him. Zander picks up the chain and locks his window as well.

I know it won't do much good if they decide to attack for real this time, but I've been trained to do what I can do, and right now this is all I can do.

But wait. There's one thing left. One thing the girls haven't counted on in their plan to corner us in my own dorm suite.

While the boys try to catch their breath, I run to my bedroom. It's deathly quiet and dark, but I don't need a light to see it's been ransacked since I was last here.

At some point after I left the suite this morning to brush my teeth and get dressed in the communal bathroom, someone—or several someones—trashed my room.

Completely.

My dead heart sinks as I race to my toppled dresser. The drawers have been tossed aside, socks everywhere.

I get on all fours near my nightstand, feeling underneath for the pager, the red button that goes straight to Dr. Haskins' line and brings the Saviors running.

I retrash the room, looking everywhere. It's not where I left it, not even *near* where I left it. I look in the closet, rip up a few floorboards, toss open whatever drawers they didn't, and still I know. Even as I'm looking, I know.

The pager is gone.

One of them, one of my Sisters, has it.

They're the only ones aware of it.

The ultimate betrayal.

I literally limp into the living room, sad beyond words, tired beyond definition.

The boys pepper me with questions.

"Lily?" Grover asks, arms crossed against his ample chest as if he's caught a chill. "Why do your friends have fangs? And why can Bianca fly? And how did you push me up four flights of stone wall with your skinny old self?"

I shake my head, beg forgiveness from Dr. Haskins, and say, "My friends, or should I say ex-friends, have fangs because they're vampires. Bianca can fly because she's been turned by a Royal, obviously, and has even more powers than the rest of us. And I can push you up four stories because, well, I'm a vampire too."

"Shut up!" He says it as if Zander's just told him he scored a personal luncheon with George Lucas next weekend.

What else can I do? We're in it now. The assignment is ruined. Our cover, my cover, is blown.

If Bianca hasn't started turning the innocent, warm-blooded students of Nightshade into vampires yet, she soon will. Now that Cara and Alice have mutinied on my butt and gone all traitor on the mission, these two boys and I are the only thing preventing an all-out infestation.

And trembling arm in arm, *boys* are exactly what they look like at the moment.

"Zander," I say firmly, shaking my head and drawing out my own fangs as proof. "I'm sorry, but that love nick last night? That came from these."

"What? You said nothing happened last night." Grover pushes him away, totally missing the point. "You lied to me, bro?"

"Uh, Grover," Zander says. "I think Lily being a vampire trumps your hurt feelings, 'kay?"

"I think you underestimate the pain of my hurt feelings, brother!"

"Silence." I hiss, fangs out and quivering, claws suddenly sharp and long. "Listen, and listen good. I am what's known as a Sister, of the Sisterhood of Dangerous Girlfriends. My job is to come to schools like Nightshade, rout out the Vamplayer, and stop you all from getting turned."

"Sisterhood of Damaged What?" Grover trembles.

"Dangerous Girlfriends." I sigh, the adrenaline fading, the claws succumbing, the fangs subsiding. "Cara and Alice are Sisters too. Or at least they were until Bianca got to them."

"You mean, those girls who tried to attack us out there are your Sisters?"

I nod. "Well, they used to be. We came here together to find the Vamplayer, but something happened. Either he turned them or he turned Bianca first and she did, but whatever it was, they've switched teams and—"

"What's a Vamplayer?" Zander asks, still looking skeptical. And who could blame them? I've had decades to absorb this stuff. These two? They're getting the condensed version in two minutes or less.

"Just what it sounds like, I'm afraid. He's part vampire, part player. His job is to seduce impressionable high school girls, turn them into vampires, and unleash them on a school, like rats on a ship, till it becomes totally infested."

Grover scratches his head, slumping on the couch, the night's physical activity too much for his normally sedentary life. "Why does he need impressionable young girls to do all that? Why doesn't he cut out the middleman and turn them all himself?"

"He can't. When a vampire turns someone, he loses some of his power. With every additional person he turns, he loses more power. But the first person he turns has the most power. Every time that person turns someone, *he* loses more."

"So, what?" Grover scratches his belly button. "If you were to turn me, or Zander here, you'd be a little weaker because of it?"

I nod. "Right. Not much but a little. But if I were to turn this whole school or even this whole floor of kids, I'd be pretty much useless. Why do you think vampires aren't always turning people left and right? They don't want to lose all their power. And it's even worse for a Royal because they have more power to lose."

"But if they have more power to lose," Zander reasons, "then isn't there more to go around?"

"You'd think so but no. The more power a vampire has, the more power he gives away each time he turns someone."

"That's why Bianca is like a vampire on steroids?" Zander paces between the couch and coffee table. "Because a Royal turned her?"

"Not normally, no. There aren't many Royals left anymore, but what I've seen Bianca do, only a Royal or someone who's been turned by a Royal can do."

"What's a Royal?" Grover says.

"A Royal is a vampire born, not bred. In other words, a Royal is not turned into a vampire like I was but is born a vampire from an Original vampire line, and they are the strongest vampires of all."

"Whoever turned Bianca had to be a Royal. Is that what you're saying?" Grover looks skeptical.

"Has to be," I hem.

"You don't sound very certain," Zander says.

"I'm not, okay? I'm not trained to fight a Royal

or even a girl turned by a Royal."

"What?" Grover squeaks. "Don't you think that's a pretty big part of your training, missy? That's like calling yourself a black belt and then, when twenty ninja assassins drop from the roof, saying you don't know kung fu!"

I frown. "Grover, the Royals are a myth. They're pure fiction, like your Jedi knights. In all my years, I've never met a vampire who's met a Royal. My headmistress has never met a vampire who's met a Royal, and she's, like, ancient. That's like me dissing you because you haven't been trained to shake hands with a Wookie."

"Who says?" he sasses, but I'm not in the mood and neither is he, really. I guess old habits just die hard. "I don't get it. If these badass Sister chicks are as good as you say, why didn't they tear us limb from limb when we were climbing up the wall?"

"And if Bianca hates you so much, why did *she* hold back?" asks Zander, still pacing. "If they wanted to get rid of us, now would be the time, don't you think? Before we tell anybody what's going on? Or call in the National Guard? Here we are, all in the same place together . . . What gives?"

I shake my head, picturing Bianca hovering

there, red hair flowing in the air like one of those underwater mermaids' wigs at some tatty Florida theme park. "I dunno. Maybe she was testing us, you know? Maybe she's trying out her powers."

The room is deathly still until Zander says, "Or maybe she's testing yours, Lily."

CHAPTER 27

Tristan literally falls into the room when I yank open the front door. I'm in such a rush to get Grover and Zander to safety that I step on him on my way out.

"Ouch!"

"What are you doing here?" My voice borders on hysteria, my fangs snapping in and out like rubber rodents in some Whac-A-Mole game at the carnival.

A sleek digital camera hangs on a thin black strap around his white linen collar, and a bag full of pricey lingerie has scattered across the floor.

Lingerie?

Grover sneaks a peek. "Dude, cross-dress much?"

Tristan stands, face red, nostrils flaring. "Nothing. I was doing nothing. What are you two doing here?"

Now that the shock of finding Tristan at my front door is wearing off, I'm instantly on high alert. I herd Zander and Grover deeper into the room.

Suddenly it all makes sense. This must be why Bianca and the girls retreated, why they let us go in the first place. It's a great plan, and even as I back-pedal I can't help but admire it. They chased us up through the back windows while Tristan, the Royal, waited for us to come out the front door.

It's a brilliant strategy, really. Too bad I'll never live to duplicate it on another mission someday.

I'm still dragging Zander and Grover along like a mother cat drags her kittens across a stream.

But we can only go so far, and soon my back is brushing curtains.

"Windows! Stay away from the windows," Grover says.

I laugh, picturing three pairs of vampire hands reaching in and snatching us out. "Good call."

We crouch in the middle of the room, me without a stake, pager, tool, or weapon of any kind. Without even my Sisters.

And with a Vamplayer standing in the doorway.

Scratch that. A Royal Vamplayer!

Hmmm, where's the Simulation for *that*, Dr. Haskins, huh?

Beside me is a small coffee table. I regard its four legs eagerly and without hesitating stomp on it, mid-table, like a frat boy squashes a beer can against his forehead to impress some skeezy coed.

It collapses on itself, sending one leg flying toward Tristan and leaving three behind. He ignores the table leg as it scoots by him and clatters out in the hallway. Ah, if only it had flown straight into his heart, this could all be over.

Instead, I'm going to have to do things the old-fashioned way.

I grab the three remaining stakes and focus on Tristan, who is busy gathering his lingerie from the hallway floor.

I hand one splintered table leg each to Grover and Zander.

"Gee, thanks." Zander twirls his like a baton.

"Yeah, awesome." Grover grins, waving his like a Groucho Marx cigar in front of his red face.

"They're not toys." I use my vampire voice: the one that growls like a sailor, roars like a bear, and cuts like a knife. "They're stakes. If something happens to me, if he gets by or finishes me, the only way to stop him is to shove this through his heart. Get it?"

"He whom?" Tristan says from the door, still blushing. A pair of lacy pink thong panties dangles from one long finger that's pointing at me accusingly.

"You, Vamplayer," I shout, advancing on him with the shattered tip of the fourth table-leg-slash-stake held shoulder high.

He makes a garbled *eek* sound in the back of his throat and stumbles farther back into the hall.

Man, is this guy staying in character until the final curtain call or *what*?

I think of potential witnesses who might walk by despite the late hour. I know I'm already dragging around too many, so I pull him back in the room, slamming the door behind us.

"Grover, get the shades. Zander, check the windows."

"You mean again?" Zander says. "For, like, the sixth ti—"

One flash from my orange-yellow eyes sets him scurrying midsentence.

They scamper around, still clutching their coffee table legs, not sure if I'm joking but not wanting to argue with a girl with a makeshift stake in her hand

and a voice like Batman's.

While they're out of the room, I plant my foot on Tristan's chest and push him onto the couch. He lands with a bounce but stays perfectly still.

I spot his pinky and the finger next to it wrapped in a do-it-yourself gauze bandage from some type of home first-aid kit. "What happened to your fingers, Vamplayer? One of those girls you turned try to return the favor?"

He snorts, looks at his fingers, and says, "If you must know, Lily, *you* did the honor. Last night, remember?"

"Man, you are really good. You mean to tell me a big, bad Vamplayer like you—a Royal no less—hasn't healed from a little wound like a sprained pinky yet? That's good, Tristan. That's rich."

"What is this Vamplayer game you keep talking about?" he says, all innocent, panties of all sizes and shapes shoved in his pockets. "And who is this Royal person? Another boy you've been seeing this week? What's your total up to by now? Hmmm? Three? Four? Fourteen?"

"Don't play dumb." I hiss, snapping back my head so that the fangs pop out. "We both know why I'm here."

His face grows pale, sweat beads on his brow

(man, this guy is slick), and he points with trembling fingers to the drool dripping off my four-inch fangs.

"Are those real?"

"Trust me, dude," Grover says from behind me, "they're all her and they're all real."

"He knows," I tell Grover without turning around, kicking Tristan's shin with a resounding thud.

He yelps.

Even Grover yelps.

I kick him again, knowing the only way to lure Tristan's fangs from his own jaw is to enrage or entice him. Pain works both ways.

"Please," the Vamplayer whimpers, rubbing his shin. "Please stop kicking me. It really, really hurts."

The panic in his voice sounds quite convincing.

The pain in his eyes looks quite real.

"Yeah, Lily," Zander says, placing a calming hand on one of my tense shoulders. "Look at the guy. He's clearly not who you think he is. I hate the dude too, but I don't want to see him in any more pain. Ease up."

"That's his game." I shrug Zander's hand off and advance on Tristan.

"What game?" Tristan whimpers, one hand covering his face, the other his bleeding shin.

"Your game." I jab at his shin with the sharp end of the stake until he squeals.

Squeals, I tell you.

I'm talking, little-girl squeals.

I'm talking, Vamplayer-who-thinks-he's-acting-like-a-human-guy squeals.

I jerk the stake, bring it to my nose, sniff. I draw it to my lips, flick my tongue, taste. I drop the stake, rush to the couch, yank open Tristan's mouth, and feel his upper gums.

Nothing.

I rip open his shirt, buttons scrambling like marbles across the hardwood floor. I place my palm on his heart and don't just feel a thump-*thump*-thump-*thump*. I feel a resounding thump-*thump*-thump-*thump*-thump-*thump*-thump-*thump*-thump-*thump*!

I leap back from the couch.

Oh no.

It can't be.

This dude is not only scared; he's . . . he's . . . human.

"Oh, God." I gasp. "Oh, Tristan, I am so, so, sooooo sorry."

But he's not listening to me. He's doing everything but listening to me. He's bleeding; he's whimpering; he's—

"Is he . . . *crying?*" Zander whispers in one ear.

"Do vampires cry?" Grover whispers in the other.

"If they could, I would." I sigh and sit on the far side of the couch from Tristan, my wrongs weighing me deep into the cushions.

Tristan whimpers, and Grover and Zander keep their distance.

All this time, I'd assumed it was Tristan who was the Vamplayer, who was the Royal.

But it's not a Vamplayer at work here at all.

It's a Vampress.

Bianca is the Royal, here to start an infestation. Somewhere along the line, she turned Alice and Cara against me. She turned them, period.

It explains everything: the overnight stays, the all-night parties, the stupid excuses.

Alice wasn't skinny-dipping that night. She was turning.

Cara wasn't in Ravens Roost with the gang. She was turning.

Bianca got to my Sisters, one by one. They needed twenty-four hours to turn completely, maybe more if a Royal like Bianca did it.

That would explain Alice's run-down look, Cara's anemic spell in PE the other day. Not to mention their extra-long fangs, more dangerous claws, and overall bad attitude.

Now it all makes perfect sense.

She knew. Bianca knew from day one. The minute she saw me in the halls, soaking wet, she saw what we were, why we were here, and what we were about to do.

She set about separating us, turning us, immediately.

First it was Alice. Then it was Cara.

Was I next?

Or was I never part of the plan to begin with?

I don't know which is scarier: to be an accomplice or a victim.

I rise on unsteady legs, my world shattered, the Sisterhood pulverized, the time at hand.

It's up to me.

Cara? Alice? They're gone, strangers, betrayers, mutineers.

It's all me. The Third Sister, the one who can't pass the Infestation Simulation even after a few dozen tries, the one who is destined to never be a Savior, try as she might.

But I can save a few before they get to me. I can save these three. These very different, very human boys.

And that's exactly what I intend to do.

"Come on." I help Tristan up.

He cringes.

"Where are we going?" Zander says.

"To finish this." I reach for the door.

"Finish what?" Grover is right behind me.

I manage a weak smile. "You know how the good guys always get one last stand at the end of all your stupid horror movies?"

"Well, not all of them are stupid but, yes, I know what you mean."

"I hope you remember how they win at the end because, fellas, this is our horror movie and this is our ending. And if we don't stop those three witches tonight, this night, then by morning Nightshade will be full of vampires."

CHAPTER 28

We limp along the halls, one Sister, three humans, at two in the morning.

The hallway is dark, with stone walls to our right side and stained glass windows to our left.

If you're picturing the last place you'd want to be in the middle of the night with three Vampresses stalking you, well, congrats—you've come to the right place!

The marble floor is hollow and dark with occasional splashes of dim yellow from weak bulbs spaced too far along the hallway to do much good.

Our footsteps echo off the walls and high ceilings, behind, before, above, making me stop every so often to be sure it's our footsteps and only our footsteps doing all that echoing.

Even though we've come this far, the hallway stretches out endlessly in front of us, like one of those rooms in *Alice in Wonderland* growing longer and longer the closer Alice gets to the door.

Tristan limps along, head a little higher now, his shame visibly turning to anger. "What's the meaning of all this?" He fiddles with the lemon-yellow thong I've wrapped around his upper calf like a tourniquet to stop the bleeding I inflicted with my makeshift stake. "You realize you're liable for all my medical bills."

"Pal," I say, towing him along as Grover leads us to the cafeteria and Zander brings up the rear, his pitiful stake held up near his shoulder, just like I taught him before leaving the dorm suite, "you'll be lucky if I'm not paying your morgue bills by the end of this. Heck, I'll be lucky if I'm paying anybody's bills by the end of this."

He stops. We all stop. "What 'this' are you referring to?" he says, hands on his hips. "I insist to know what's going on here. If you don't explain yourself, I'll be forced to call my father in Europe and—"

A swift whack interrupts him, doubling him over.

Zander stands over him triumphantly, his stake raised high.

Grover yanks Tristan's wallet out of his back pocket and hands me his driver's license. His Pennsylvania driver's license.

Tristan glares.

"Tristan *Whitehead*?" I stare at a paler, younger, thinner Tristan circa a few years ago. "Of 1927 Bayshore Drive, Pittsburgh, Pennsylvania?"

He steps forward. "I can explain."

"I don't get it." I stop him with the spiky end of my stake pointed at his chest. "The phony accent, the long hair, the manicured fingers, the picnic basket, the blood wine. That's all expensive."

Grover yanks one pair of pink panties out of one of Tristan's pockets. "I know how he affords it."

"Shut up, water buffalo."

Zander thwacks Tristan on the head with his stake.

"Tristan runs this website, see. *Nymphets of Nightshade.* He told me about it once, bragged about it, actually, but I never believed him at the time. Now it all makes sense. He sneaks into girls' rooms late at night, slips them some mickey, and dresses them up in sexy lingerie. Then he snaps pictures and uploads them to his site. The girls' families pay to take them down, and he pockets the cash."

Tristan's blush proves Grover right, though he seems hardly fazed by the admission. "Some of us work in cafeterias to pay our tuition," he explains calmly, all former traces of his European accent suddenly gone. "Some of us are more resourceful. That's all."

"You pig!" I shove him toward the cafeteria, and we march on. "You absolute moronic, presumptive pig. That's why you were at my door when I came barging out? That's why you had that camera around your neck? And a bag full of panties? I should gut you right here and—"

Grover's the first one to spot them. "Uh, Lily, something . . . Make that several somethings seem to be following us."

I check the hall behind us.

Zander shrugs, looking in the other direction and finding nothing in front of us either.

"Not in here." Grover points his stake. "Out. There."

We stop and face the stained glass windows.

This hallway is part cathedral, part monastery, part tomb. Every sound is amplified, every sight is doubled, every breath takes a minute to reach the high arched ceiling.

Moonlight plus streetlights filter through the

glass, both weakly.

It's like someone's on the roof, dangling Halloween witch cutouts from a fishing pole. The shadows zip around at first, unnaturally fast, then seem to hover.

But I know that can't be right. In training we're taught to soar, not to hover. Soaring is like climbing, just without your hands or feet. But the longest I've ever lasted in midair is about fifteen seconds. Cara and Alice might last longer: twenty-five seconds, maybe thirty.

These shadows are hanging, one arm dangling from the arctic, stone roof, the other seeming to point.

I can see their outlines and make them out: Bianca in the middle looking distorted through a purple stained glass scene of women eating grapes on a lounge chair.

To the left, Alice, hair wild, claws long in the filtering light, looks garish through a window depicting high, rolling green fields.

To the right of Bianca dangles Cara, her features distinct yet gaudy behind a field of red roses, her mouth open. In profile, her fangs are like chopsticks jutting from her upper jaw.

"They're playing with us again," I say through

tight lips. "Keep moving. Fast, before they want to come inside."

We scramble ahead double time, each of us leaning closer to the rough stone walls. Our footsteps scrape, our breathing heavy and sour.

Even Tristan is heeling, no longer complaining, his limp more pronounced.

The shadows follow us, their outlines severe.

"What is that?" Tristan hobbles along, sweat dripping from his forehead.

"Not *what*," I say. "Who. And one of them is your girlfriend."

"Sable?" he asks.

I smack him on the shoulder. "No! And who's Sable?"

"Minx?" He wheezes, lurching along like Quasimodo in the bell tower.

Another slap. "How many girlfriends do you have, Tristan? It's Bianca, you fool."

"Out there? Why? How?"

"Have you even been paying attention?" Zander asks, still moving steadily, his breath hot on my neck, his hands gently shoving me along, his long legs outpacing mine every now and again. "We're under attack, idiot. By vampires. Three of them. And they're out there. Limp along, playboy. You're holding us up."

I smirk over my shoulder at his newly macho tone, trying not to laugh at the pitiful coffee table leg stake in his trembling hand.

The scratching comes, horrible nails against beautiful stained glass.

Reflexively, we pause.

First, one Vampress scrapes with her long claws, leaving deep gashes in the crumbling, quaking, dense glass.

Then the next, her fingernails starting at the very top of the window and screeching all the way down like forty pounds of chalk on the world's biggest chalkboard. Chips and rusty solder crumble, scattering like pebbles on the hallway floor.

By the time the third Vampress starts, chunks of beautiful, antique, no doubt expensive stained glass are falling to the floor.

"It's like during the Zombie Film Fest," Zander whispers breathlessly in my ear, so close I can almost feel his lips. "It wasn't a bird at all."

I shake my head. "No, it wasn't." I turn to him, hunks of stained glass scattering on the floor, the rush of chill air from outside streaming through the cracks.

"You were protecting us, weren't you?" He cocks

his head slightly.

"I was trying then. I'm trying now."

I hear hissing and see Bianca through a hole in the glass.

More hissing. Alice claws at the lead holding the stained glass pieces together.

On the other side of Bianca, Cara is systematically yanking out glass fragments, dropping them to the ground below.

It's beginning.

All of it.

Right here.

Right now.

"Run," I shout.

For once, I don't have to tell them twice.

CHAPTER 29

The cafeteria is empty and desolate and so, so big. The doors swing shut, and I still hear the muffled scraping, the trembling of walls, the cracking of thick stained glass echoing through the halls. I know it won't be long before they claw their way through, stiff, dark toenails scurrying toward us on the marble floor.

"Here?" Tristan says. "This is where you choose to have our big standoff with the Bitches of Eastwick?"

Grover snorts.

"Not here." I point to the silent kitchen doors. "There."

The floor seems to lengthen. We pass rows and

rows of empty tables.

What will happen if this doesn't work, if we don't find some way to trap, conquer, or stop these beasts?

We reach the swinging doors, rush through.

Grover flips on lights as we go. No need for hiding anymore.

The vampires are surely through the windows and right around the corner.

I stand in the middle of the room, get my bearings, and try to figure out where Tristan can do the least damage.

I shove him to the floor in the corner near the dishwasher.

The dishwasher where I met Grover and Zander when this crazy week began.

It seems like yesterday. It seems like ten years ago.

"Stay!" I order.

Tristan crouches, knees against his chest, as if he can roll into the cabinets at his side.

"Do not move."

He grumbles.

Grover and Zander both join me at the metal cutting counter in the middle of the room.

"What now?" Grover pants and rubs sweat off his forehead with one beefy arm.

I point to the utensils, the tools, the bowls, and the pots and pans. "Now we get to work. We need two things: wood and garlic. Zander, gather the rolling pins, the soup spoons, anything long I can sharpen into a stake. Grover, find the garlic, as much of it as you can. Just keep it away from me. Hurry. We don't have much time."

I grab a paring knife, short but solid and thick, and sharpen the coffee table leg I've been lugging. When it's done I ask Grover for his, then Zander.

Wood cuttings flutter to the floor, making a small, uneven pile at my feet.

Grover rummages through cabinets, a huge pantry, drawers, and gleaming metal shelves lined with huge jars of tomato sauce and industrial-sized ketchup barrels.

A small pile of garlic grows on top of the table next to the sharpened rolling pins and wooden spoon stakes: garlic cloves, minced garlic in big jars, garlic paste in shiny metal tins that look imported like Tristan's blood sausage.

My eyes begin watering, my skin itching even from a few feet away, like a skunk has sprayed someone nearby or the room is filling with acrid smoke.

"You'll have to handle the garlic," I warn them,

shoving the pile away with the blunt end of a rolling pin stake and even then feeling my fingertips sizzle. "I can't touch it. I shouldn't even be near it."

Grover pulls some toward him, shoving some cloves and a smaller jar or two in his jeans pockets, and Zander does the same.

I watch them work diligently, not speaking, not looking at each other, as if to share a glance would prove too terrifying or drive them, or even me, insane.

I do this every day, train for this every week, test for it every month, and these guys are just, well, guys. Geeks, really. Big old softies doing what they're told, going on autopilot, listening to me because I've got fangs.

I know what's clawing through those windows, what's skulking our way, will kill them if they get the chance, will tear them limb from limb without mercy, without thought, sucking them dry. As if they're not Zander, not Grover, not boys with hopes and dreams and healthy, beating hearts.

I want to warn them of the danger to life and limb, to say one of them—maybe all of them, all of us—may not survive. But what kind of strategy is that? I should be giving them a pep talk, like some football coach during halftime or four-star general before a big battle. But while I can't exactly share the truth about the danger they're in, I can't outright lie to them either.

Instead I stay silent, head bent to the work, stretching the time, making us worthy of the task.

I hear fumbling in the corner. Tristan leans against a counter in the corner, scavenging through a cabinet full of grape juice. "Will this help?" he asks, almost meekly, holding up a bottle in his trembling hand.

I look at the shiny foil wrapper and groan. "These are vampires, not third graders. I'm not going to ask them to take naps and pour fancy grape juice in their sippy cups."

"Are you quite through? This is communion wine, dear, for our humble chapel."

I shrug, still sharpening, no time to spare, least of all to soothe poor Tristan's ego.

"It's a little too late to pray, but if you think it will help, be my guest."

From behind, where Grover's busy dipping sharpened stakes into a reeking tin of garlic oil, he says urgently, "No, he means it's blessed."

"As in?"

"As in it's holy." Tristan smiles, carrying a case

of bottles from the bottom cabinet to our stash on the counter.

"Holy communion wine." I smile, patting him with a free hand, and pick up another rolling pin to sharpen. "Way to make yourself useful."

He ignores the jab, studying the bottles of wine as if he's measuring how much they might help the cause.

"Now," Zander says, smiling and holding a sharpened stake, "this is shaping up to be a fight."

Yeah, a short one.

CHAPTER 30

The cafeteria doors burst open, and even I get chills. The sound is so expected; we've been waiting for it for like ten minutes. Yet it's so unexpected, too, so loud and rough and unforgiving, like the vampires themselves.

Grover looks through the grimy kitchen window and says, unnecessarily, "They're here."

"You think?" Zander says, then joins him at the window.

I'm shoving stakes in every possible belt loop. "All three?"

Zander and Grover answer in unison, "Yup."

"Turn around," I say. When they do, I toss

multiple stakes at them.

They grab them clumsily, and two clatter to the floor.

No, wait, only one falls to the floor. I watch it land near Zander's feet before he leans to pick it up and shove it through a belt loop. (Good boy.)

So . . . what's the other clattering noise?

Is that? Really? Yes, it is; it's the vent cover from the ceiling right above our heads.

"Tristan"—I follow Zander's gaze toward the nearest air vent, where Tristan's bloody leg disappears—"get down here and fight like a man."

"Fight your own battles." We hear him scuttling away crab-like in the air ducts above our heads. The sound is far from quiet, like two coffee cans slamming together over and over again.

"Can you believe that?" Zander says, looking at the grate on the floor.

I hear claws on tile on the other side of the kitchen door, sense the vampires getting closer, closer. "Put that back, Zander, before they get here."

"What, you're going to let him run?" He stands on the chopping table and wedges the vent cover in with the fat end of his palm.

"If he won't fight anyway, it's better not to have him around. Get down before they see you."

He jumps to the floor.

The double doors swing open, slamming into cupboards on either side and sending pots and pans and jars of oregano skittering on the rust-colored tiles. The sound is at once grating and shocking.

Grover and Zander scramble to my side. The pungent odor from their garlic-tipped stakes makes my eyes water and my throat tighten.

I tread forward, a stake in each hand, and crouch in a thrust and parry stance I learned my first week at the Academy. My legs are limber, back loose, sharp claws stretching from fingertips, fangs sliding deliciously from upper gums, pores open, senses on red alert.

Bianca stands in front, radiant in a black leather track suit open at the collar like an action figure version of herself.

Cara stands to her left, sleek in all white.

Alice wears red and lots of it.

"Amazing"—I hope they won't hear the warble in my voice—"that you three found the time to coordinate your look. Bianca, I guess that makes you Josie. And these two are the Pussycats?"

Apparently Grover's the only one to get the joke. He smirks.

"You have two choices." Bianca feigns boredom,

peering at Grover first, then Zander. "Give up or die horrible, excruciating deaths."

"We're not giving up."

She hasn't actually looked at me yet. "I wasn't talking to you. You're already dead and, besides, I'll let the Council of Ancients deal with you later."

"The Council? What for? I haven't done anything wrong."

Bianca smiles. I swear she's had her frickin' hair done! It's like she's ready for prom or something. Who takes time out of a Vampire Armageddon to get their damn hair done?

"Why, trying to kill a Royal, of course. The Academy might not take such infractions seriously, but the Council certainly does."

"The Council started the Academy," I remind her. "They wanted us to stop witches like you from turning whole schools like this. That's why they started the Sisterhood in the first place."

"Be that as it may, being a Sister doesn't exempt you from the Vampire Book of Laws."

"Vampires have laws?" Grover says.

"Silence, human!"

The way Alice snaps is so ridiculous even I want to snicker. "What law is that?" I say instead.

"Why, the very first one: thou shalt not wound a Royal."

"Hmm, well, that clashes with law number two: thou shalt not kill an Innocent."

"Innocents are children. Everyone knows that."

"Zander is innocent. Grover is innocent." I almost add Tristan, but that would make her too suspicious. I wonder if he's listening somewhere overhead. If he's feeling guilty for running out on us when we need him the most. Or if he already slid down a laundry chute somewhere far, far away, hot-wired a van in the employee parking lot, and is cruising to safety (and the nearest strip club).

"We'll let the Council sort it out. Hand over the humans, or we'll be forced to break any number of laws by tearing each of you limb from limb."

I hold up my pitiful two stakes, garlic stinging my eyes. "Just try it," I say, stepping forward.

"Seize them," Bianca says.

Cara and Alice stalk.

I leap onto the table, kicking several bowls of minced garlic square at their faces.

Cara, always the fastest of the two, ducks in time. Behind her the minced garlic explodes on the wall in a cartoon splat that instantly fills the room with a vampire version of tear gas.

The fumes are noxious and violent. It's all I can do to stand upright.

Alice, who always preferred texting to training, ducks more slowly and winds up with a faceful. She gags and coughs and sputters, retching violently.

I leap from the table and shove one of the stakes into her chest, missing her heart by a fraction of an inch.

She hisses and kicks me across the kitchen, swiping frantically at her skin to get the garlic off and the stake out.

I land in water near the giant dishwasher, shake my head, and kneel. I stand, grabbing the nozzle to spray, if only to confuse them, but drop it instantly.

It clangs to the floor, the sound echoing loudly off the walls.

"Like I said, Lily," Bianca says calmly, her long, quivering fangs bared at Zander's throat, "give up or let these boys die horrible, excruciating deaths."

Cara has Grover in a similarly compromising position.

Alice retches on the floor, her hands flat and trembling on the tiles, her back alternately arching and dipping as she tries to exorcise the garlic fumes from her already singed lungs.

I approach, dropping stakes from my belt loop one by one. They're of no use to me now anyway. The last one rattles to the rust-colored tiles, and I raise my hands.

Cara backs through the kitchen doors into the cafeteria, dragging Grover with her.

Bianca follows with Zander in tow, leaving Alice behind to fend for herself.

I heel like a good little dog.

Because that's what we're trained to do when a human life is in danger.

I t comes to this. A simple standoff in the middle of the
night, the school sleeping around us quietly, its fate in
the balance here in this large, Lysol-smelling cafeteria.

Around us the tables seem to stretch for miles,
empty chairs like tombstones lined silently next to
each other.

"Fine," I say, hands up. "Release them."

Bianca snickers, tossing her head back, flipping
her hair. Her claw never moves from where it's held
against Zander's soft, vulnerable neck. "In due time.
First we'll have to make sure you get to the Council
safely, of course, and after that we'll let them—"

"You know the Council will never let these boys

live, not once they've seen where the Ancients dwell."

Bianca looks unconcerned. "That's a risk we'll have to—"

Screams from the kitchen cut her off. Through the red double doors, Alice stumbles, melting from head to toe. Slabs of her skull are already visible, one jawbone poking out from shrinking flesh, teeth clattering to the floor. Smoke sizzles from her hair, her ears, her shoulders, her thighs, burning from an invisible fire even I can't see. Shoulders drip into biceps drip into elbows drip into forearms. Like a chicken left too long in the oven, her skin literally falls from her bones.

"Alice," Cara shrieks, seeming ready to drop Grover and run to her ex-Sister.

Bianca silences her with a hiss.

I feel Cara's pain. I want to join her as well, but too much has happened between us this week for me to feel much regret over Alice's current, bubbling misfortune.

"But . . . but garlic can't do that." I stand my ground, desperate, anxious to use this development to free Zander, to reach Grover.

"No," Cara says, loosening her grip on Grover, "it can't."

The room grows still.

Alice sizzles, melting into the floor like the Wicked Witch of the West.

Maybe she's having an allergic reaction.

Or maybe that's how Royals, or vampires turned by Royals, react to garlic.

I hear clanging in the kitchen, a pot falling to the floor.

We all flinch, even Zander.

Then silence.

Several yards away, the red doors remain still.

Bianca watches carefully, moving behind Zander.

The doors fly open, and two bottles sail across the room, careening end over end, whispering through the air above us.

"No," Tristan shouts from the kitchen doorway, triumphantly, his hands empty, "garlic doesn't do that, but holy wine sure does." His expression is ecstatic, his arms wide, his shirt grimy from the air ducts high above, dried blood staining the yellow thong tourniquet on his leg.

Cara ducks again, her reflexes right on cue but not in time.

Not this time.

The bottle hits her head with a solid thunk,

exploding in a red gush of sacramental wine and searing her beautiful skin.

Grover sees his opportunity, slips away from Cara, and instinctively plunges the stake from his belt loop into her gurgling chest. It strikes gold, piercing her long-dead heart.

While he backs away excitedly, she shrieks until her vocal cords melt, waving her arms wildly. The skin peels away, and the clean white bones poke through. Skin and muscle and cartilage slither onto the floor between gushes of blood expelling from her body to escape the consecrated wine.

I stop looking when I can see clear through her rib cage to the cafeteria table behind her. I hang my head in shame, in fear, in anger, in grief.

I hear shrieking and realize it's me.

I want to help, but even as I cross the room I know it's too late.

Eventually all that's left at Grover's feet is a pile of bones and pus, half bubbling, half spreading across the cafeteria floor.

Another bottle lands at Bianca's feet, searing her toes, igniting her heels in flames. She stumbles back, hissing violently, a pool of wine chasing her across the cafeteria floor. Unlike everything else she's done to date, her movements are frantic, detached, unpre-dictable, unwieldy. She's like a housewife screeching at a mouse in some black-and-white fifties sitcom.

Unfortunately, she's not alone.

I'm already in pursuit, watching Zander's fear as Bianca's wicked claws dig into his shoulder.

She drags him toward the doors.

"Zander," I shout.

Another volley of bottles sails through the air. Like beer bottles in a bar fight, they splash the walls on either side of the cafeteria's double doors. The hallowed wine splatters Bianca's face and scores her to the bone.

She screams, her hair on fire before she pats it out with one hand and tugs Zander into the hall with the other.

I rush to Grover, who stands amidst a pile of what used to be Cara.

Sweet Cara.

I'm careful of the wine at my feet. Even a drop could burn through me like acid, taking me out of this game before it even starts.

I rip a strip of cloth from the hem of my shirt and wrap it around my hand, hesitating. My wrapped fingers linger over what's left of Cara's carcass.

I reach into her putrid flesh to grab Grover's stake from where it's fallen into her ribs.

"Gross," Grover says.

"I know." I grunt, wiping it off on my pants. "But we might need this for late—"

Just then, something metallic-sounding rattles across the floor.

I look, rush to it, wipe still steaming flesh from its digital display, and exhale.

It's Cara's and must have fallen out of one of her pockets. I might not have found it otherwise or, in my shock and panic, thought to look.

"What is it?" Tristan says, handing Grover a wine bottle.

I hold up the pager, my finger pressed firmly on the red button in the center. "Salvation."

CHAPTER 32

We follow the growing blood trail through the surprisingly silent halls. Grover is breathless, tired, a gore-stained stake in one hand, a bottle of sacred wine in the other.

Beside me, Tristan grins, hoisting his own stake and wine bottle for effect. "Some performance back there, huh, Lily?" he says as if he's just entertained fifty thousand screaming fans.

I cluck my tongue against the roof of my mouth. "Yeah, Tristan, sure. Why not? We could have used it before they kidnapped Zander and lured him to his death, but whatevs."

He seems offended. "I saved the day, did I not?"

"Yeah, sure, you saved the day. I'm very grateful, but we don't leave anyone behind, okay? The day's not over. Not until we get Zander back."

"Forget him." He pauses near a fire alarm.

I stop, if only to give Grover a moment to catch his breath. "We can't forget him. We *won't* forget him. Fine, you don't care about Zander; we get that. But in case you've forgotten, this school is full of hims and hers. If we don't stop Bianca, innocent kids will get slaughtered, drained, and turned. Do you care about *them*?"

His impatient expression makes it clear that, no, he really doesn't. "The exit is that way," he says, pointing in the opposite direction of Bianca's blood trail. "The school is in danger. Look at this beautiful fire alarm. I say we pull it, alert everybody, and wait for the cops. Let them take care of it. We're kids, remember?"

What is this guy on?

Seriously?

Does he honestly think this is over?

That we can walk away and whistle a tune while a Royal runs amok at Nightshade?

"The cops are twenty-five minutes away, Tristan! They're also *human*. They haven't seen what you've seen. I've been here before, okay? It will take them two hours to believe us, and by then Bianca and Zander will be long gone."

"Let them be," he says. "We are alive, no? Zander is . . . is done for, I'm afraid."

Rough hands pin him to the hard stone wall. Grover, red-faced and standing on tiptoes, says through gritted teeth, "Zander is my friend, you big, phony, pompous jerk, and none of us, you included, leave without him. Got that?" He shoves him one last time for good measure before releasing him.

Tristan coughs and sputters. "Of course, my friend. It was merely a suggestion." But his eyes say otherwise.

I pledge to watch him more closely.

We silently move away from the fire alarm, away from the cafeteria, away from safety, and willingly toward danger.

And hopefully a rescue.

The trail disappears where two hallways begin.

I bend to the floor, studying the end of the smear.

Grover grunts, kneeling by my side. "Looks like she wiped it up." He points to a clean swipe mark that signals the end of Bianca's trail as clearly as if she'd used a giant eraser to blot out her name.

"So we wouldn't know which way she was going," I murmur somewhat approvingly. "Smart. So where do these halls lead?"

Everything has happened so fast and gone so wrong. I've never had time to scope out this particular section of the school until now.

Grover looks down both halls, scratching his curly black hair. "I have no idea."

"That is because you are a techie," Tristan says. He's not leaning to the trail but still standing above us, smirking, a stake slid through his belt loop, the bottom of his wine bottle resting against his thigh.

"Trekkie," Grover corrects without looking up.

"No, because you are a technical person and you only live in the computer lab in the technical wing. These halls are for active people. One leads to the varsity locker rooms, the other to the indoor pool."

I stand. "She's smart; she wants us to split up."

Tristan says, "That is a bad idea."

"Really?" I snap. "Thanks for the input."

Grover struggles to get up, and I drag him to a standing position. A tad forcefully (okay, a lot forcefully), he says, "But we have to, Lily. We don't have time to mess around. She's probably at the pool already. Let me take Tristan, and I'll—"

"I don't trust Tristan," I say, not caring that the guy himself is standing right behind me, sniffling.

Grover shrugs and lopes in the opposite direction. "Fine," he calls out. "I'll go myself. I've always wanted to see the girls' locker room anyway. You know, other than on the girls' locker room webcam, that is."

"Grover," I shout, but he's already too far away and I don't have time to chase a practically grown man into the locker rooms.

"Come on. Let's go."

But Tristan stands firm. "Why should I go with a woman who doesn't trust me?"

"Because if you don't, I'll shove this stake where the sun don't shine. That's why."

He follows me resolutely, the wine in his bottle sloshing, the glass clinking against his expensive belt buckle.

The auditorium at our feet is large, dank, and dark.

I wouldn't flip on the lights except I need Tristan's help, and he has to see. One after the other, the lights flicker on like a wave spreading across the ceiling some three or four stories above, illuminating an Olympic-sized pool, several Jacuzzis, and numbered rooms for what look like saunas.

"Look for wet tiles," I say, nose wrinkling at the scent of chlorine permeating the air. "Discarded towels. She'll want to get wet to stop the holy wine from doing any more damage."

"Surely she can't have gotten far?" he says, inspecting the pool deck nonetheless. "Last time we saw her, she was practically melting."

"She's a Royal, Tristan. She's probably already healing as we speak. The water will help, but she doesn't necessarily need it for her cells to begin regenerating."

I spot a puddle on the pool deck and get hopeful, and then a drop of water splashes on my shoulder.

It's from a leak in the ceiling high overhead.

I keep moving, keep lurking, the serene surface of the pool water placid and relaxing.

You know, if you're not smack-dab in the middle of Vampire Armageddon, that is.

I stop and put my hand on the floor, trying to sense the Royal. Nothing.

I stand, recognizing the sound of silence, the sound of absence.

"She's not here." I clutch Tristan's collar and drag him back into the empty hallway.

"Maybe the lockers," he says, back to using his stilted Euro-speak.

We start walking, only to hear sneakers squeaking in our direction.

Grover rounds a corner and stumbles into view. "What happened?"

His face is flushed. "I looked everywhere. Girls' lockers, girls' shower. She's not there."

I look down the hall we came from, where the blood trail ends. "Where would that hall have led if we'd gone the other direction?"

"What, you think she circled around?" Grover asks.

"Like the hunters do," Tristan says, nodding, "when they follow their tracks back through the snow."

Who is this guy, and what has he done with Tristan?

"Where does it lead, Grover?" I say, impatient.

"The chapel, but why would she go there?"

CHAPTER 33

Bianca is praying, smoke still rising from her ripe young body, half her expensive, color-coordinated clothes torn from the searing heat, her skin underneath already puckered pink.

She's already healing. In some places, she's already healed.

I think of my finger pressed firm on the red send button of Dr. Haskins' beeper and pray it went through, pray they're on their way.

"Hey," Grover whispers, apparently not wanting to disturb Bianca. "I thought you weren't supposed to be in here. Aren't you supposed to burst into flames or something?"

I roll my eyes despite the grim circumstances. "Don't believe everything you read."

Tristan stands at the door, and I can see his gaze darting down the hall to safety.

"Look," I say, my voice low but not out of respect for Bianca's silent prayers. "Run away or stay. I don't care. But we could use your help, and it would be nice to count on you for once. Make up your mind, will you?"

"Okay, okay." He groans, following us in reluctantly.

Bianca is kneeling at the altar, her head bowed. Even her hair is growing itself back out. From across the room, I can hear it: the sound thread makes scratching through fabric, follicles and long red strands extending through her scalp.

I watch the boys' faces, but apparently they can't hear it. Frankly, I wish I couldn't.

I can see she's weak but not down for the count, wounded but far from vanquished.

"What are you praying for?" I interrupt, walking forward boldly because this is the part where I finish her off.

She doesn't look up. "Your soul, of course."

"Where is he?" I ask, ignoring her repartee, trying to sound strong.

"Safe and sound." She points behind me. Thin smoke, almost like a mist, rises in coiling tendrils from her fingers as her skin continues to regenerate.

I guess it's true what I've always heard about Royals: they are badass!

In a wading pool behind me, Zander rests nearly up to his shoulders in holy water.

The liquid comes gurgling from a copper fountain shaped like a winged cherub pouring a wine jug into the pool at Zander's feet.

Well, that doesn't look very hazardous at all.

Zander's not a vampire, so he's not in any danger from the holy water, right? If this is her big, shocking finale, then she's not very good at this because—

His posture looks awkward. I peer in. His hands are bound behind him, pushing his spine upward and his head slightly back.

His curly hair is wet in the back, his broad forehead waxy, his eyes glassy, his clothes soaked, his lips sputtering as water laps up and ebbs back, the fountain gushing, splattering him all around.

He looks dazed, like maybe she conked him on the head when she dumped him in there.

The pool is filling quickly, the water racing up his chest and, gently, to his shoulders. His ankles are tied up. He can't move, and the pool is already three-quarters full.

"No worries." Grover ambles over. "I'll just snatch him out, and we'll be on our way."

Before I can move, before I can blink, Bianca rises from the altar, sails across the room, and grabs Grover by his hair.

There is a moment there, trapped in time, when she holds him so effortlessly, so lightly, it's like she's in some black market bazaar holding a shrunken head.

He squirms.

It's all happening so fast.

He flashes me a panicked look.

I flash one back.

It's like Bianca's had enough. She flicks her wrist and tosses him against the chapel wall.

Hard.

He hits with a deep, wet smack and slides down the wall, wheezing. His head leaves a straight trail of blood, almost like it's been applied by a paint roller.

The slap of his skull on marble still ringing, the holy water in Zander's pool swashing, I'm momentarily paralyzed.

I gasp and sail to him.

I kneel, feeling for a pulse, knowing I'm vulnerable

facing away from Bianca, aware that this is exactly what she wants.

Tristan has my back. I look over my shoulder to see him react quickly, holding the bottle of holy wine above his head to douse her in it.

But again she's too quick.

Bianca grabs his arm unnaturally, like you'd grab a porcelain doll, the kind with cloth arms and no bones.

I hear something snap, watch Tristan's face erupt in pain, and the bottle drops harmlessly to the floor.

Before it can soak her feet or scald her toes or sizzle through what's left of her tattered clothing, she yanks Tristan by the hair into an alcove just a few feet above the holy water pool.

He's over six feet tall, at least one hundred seventy pounds of straight-up, stone cold muscle, and she carries him like a plaything. She soars, and his legs dangle and swing.

He yelps but doesn't scream. He struggles but only until she threatens him, one long, pointy claw at his throat.

She nestles him on her lap, like a mother nursing a babe.

The alcove is high and deep, cast in shadows

from the moonlight pouring in through the tiny chapel's stained glass ceiling.

I could reach it and save him if I had time, but already I hear Zander coughing and spluttering in the pool, the water reaching his throat.

I shake my head. All that training and I'm nothing against a Royal.

Scratch that.

Next to nothing.

All those Simulations, all those stupid stakes spitting out of idiotic walls, and they never said anything about having to save three humans all at once against a force so powerful it can repair itself—and kill your friends—right before your very eyes.

Grover breathes raggedly. His skin is pale and slick. His eyes flicker but never open.

I feel the pulse at his neck (I'm an expert in the jugular), and it feels like a hose that's run out of water, growing slack beneath my fingers. There is a silence about him, a stillness, that I try to deny.

"Grover!" I shake him until at last he coughs himself to life.

He smiles and gasps and moves his lips, but he's out of funny lines. The jokes have all run dry.

The water must be up to Zander's chin by now.

Tristan whimpers in the alcove, where Bianca gloats. Grover struggles to draw in one breath, then two.

Then no more.

There will not be a third.

The light goes out of his eyes.

His massive chest droops into his even bigger belly.

I wait for him to gasp, to rise, to cough, to laugh.

That's how this is supposed to end: we all get up, we all walk away, we all go home.

Not for Grover.

There is no gasp, no wink to say he's faking it, no Hollywood ending, no zombie hand reaching up from his grave.

There is only stillness and softness and eternal, endless sadness.

I scream, cry, rage, hiss, and fly—fangs popping, claws pouncing—to the alcove above.

It is a soaring leap, like Michael Jordan in all those old-school YouTube videos from his glorious Air Jordan days. My chest is out, my legs bent slightly, my arms at my sides, my head back, the air playing with my long black hair.

I am blind to my vulnerability, blinder still to the danger. I see only my enemy, fangs bared, claws out, Tristan squirming in her lap as we prepare to clash.

It never gets that far.

She kicks me once in the ribs so hard I land all the way across the chapel before I know what's happened. I'm in a pile of pews, sharp edges in my bones, tears in my skin. It takes everything I have not to fly up there and try it all over again.

Instead I stand.

I walk.

I run beneath the alcove, to the side of the wading pool.

"You didn't have to kill him." I hiss up at her. "He never did anything to you."

She sneers, tousling Tristan's long hair as if she hasn't just taken a human life, as if she isn't about to take another. "No, but *you* did. I told you I'd take something you cared about. Now you know how it feels."

"I knew how it felt. You already took two things I cared about."

She shrugs. "You should thank me."

"Whatever for?"

"Now your choice is even easier." Bianca settles against the alcove, as if the only thing missing from her big entertainment is a bag of popcorn and an ice-cold soda. "You can choose to save Zander, which of course will result in horrible pain, maybe even death, for you. Or you can choose to save Tristan here, which of course will cause you no pain at all."

"I'm fine, Lily," Tristan mutters.

She scratches his shoulder as a reward. I watch fresh blood poke out through the tear in his white linen shirt.

I judge the distance between where I'm standing and where Bianca is holding Tristan, then watch as the water licks Zander's pursed lips.

The weight of the world is heavy on my shoulders, my dead heart wracked with sadness for poor Grover, who never got a second act or any last words, who died quickly and needlessly.

"Please," I whimper, even though I know it's exactly what she wants me to do. Even though I know it has zero chance of working. "Please don't make me choose. Go. Leave here. I won't tell anyone. I won't even chase you to your next school. Just let these boys live. They've done nothing to you."

"And I've done nothing to *you*, Lily." She caresses Tristan's head like Dr. Evil with his hairless cat in those Austin Powers movies. "And yet here you are, ruining my plans, upsetting my world. Look what you've done to my relationship. Why, Tristan here is afraid of me. Aren't you, dear? And all because of you. Tell me, Lily, why should I show you a courtesy you're unwilling to show me?"

I walk toward the wading pool. I have to.

"I'm . . . I'm sorry, Tristan," I say even as I make my choice.

"It's okay," he shouts. "I understand. I know I've been a jerk. I know I ran out on you when you needed me most. W-w-why should you ch-choose me?"

"Ah." Bianca bares her fangs. "Poor Tristan. Well, dear, I guess it's you and me then. You know, being a vampire's not so bad. Especially when a Royal turns you. Why, in no time at all you'll be stronger than Lily here. I imagine that might come in quite handy as you seek revenge for the choice she's made here today."

I can't hear her anymore. I'm in the wading pool reaching in to drag Zander out, the sound of my skin frying and the holy water bubbling. It's like acid, if acid were on crack and crack were on speed and speed were full of double-sided razor blades attached to an electric toothbrush.

Every drop is a slice against my skin, shredding it like jerky. It's searing when it touches and bubbles. It's like sticking your finger in a fireplace, holding it until you can't take it anymore, and then jumping in and taking a seat on the hottest log.

I don't scream.

I can't.

I've given her too much of my fear, my shame, already. I won't give her any more. Royal or not, she's gotten all she will from me.

With the last of my strength, I hoist Zander out of the water. I feel my own blood pour from my skin and see Tristan's neck gouged and gory too. Drops splatter the alcove and drip down the walls of this once pristine and sacred chapel.

His hair hangs in his blanched face. His gaze is far away, which makes me feel better somehow.

Except that my skin is on fire and my fingers and toes are smoking. The pain wells up in me, burning from the outside in, boiling my organs, congealing my blood, fusing my cells, closing off my lungs. I'm panting. My skin is melting, dribbling down my arms, my legs.

I dump Zander onto the chapel floor and pull at the ties binding his hands, eager to free him, to tell him to run, but my fingertips are bony and sharp, the flesh all but eaten away. I nearly faint at the sight.

Instead I crumble next to him, lying in a heap of my own goo.

The stained glass ceiling of the chapel shatters

into a thousand tiny pieces.

Eight figures sail to the floor, each dressed in red leather. With crossbows already pointed, they silence Bianca with simple precision. Eight razor-sharp arrows plunge into her heart like darts shoved into a bull's-eye.

If only they'd been sixty seconds earlier.

CHAPTER 34

I wake up in the Tank. I've never been in it before. The Tank is just that: a large, clear coffin filled with special healing waters, their exact properties known only to the Ancients. Heavy metal bolts fix the four sides and bottom to each other. Kind of like a fish tank (from hell), it has no lid.

It sits atop a steel platform from which tubes and dials and hoses and cords spill out willy-nilly, continually filling the container with healing jets of antibiotics and who knows what else.

The only light that penetrates comes from rows of soft-white lightbulbs strung overhead.

It's kept in the basement of the Academy, three

stories underground, behind locked doors. Special vampires, not quite Ancients, not quite the rest of us, carry out the sole task of regulating the Tank, but no one dares enter unless accompanied by Dr. Haskins herself.

Mostly it's for the Saviors when they return from battle, scarred and torn, bleeding and broken. I've never known of one of the Sisters using—or needing—it before.

I've heard rumors about the Tank. We all have. It burns worse than the holy water. You have to stay in there for months, maybe years. Some kids never make it out. The shock alone can kill you if you're not prepared. All of this, I've heard.

But once you're in it, well, it's not so bad. Unless I'm in so much shock I can't tell how horrible it really is. Unless I'm already gone and this is all some very precise and detailed dream.

I blink twice to make sure.

Yup, same rows of bulbs, acrylic Tank walls, plain white cinder block beyond that. Same familiar face staring down at me.

Dr. Haskins smiles cautiously, her blonde hair up and severe, her rectangular glasses near my face.

For a second the image is so strong, the memory

so vivid, the déjà vu so powerful it's like I'm in my old room, lying on the floor, my mother next to me, a stake in her heart, blood pouring from my throat, Rick Springfield winking down at me from my poster on the wall.

It was Dr. Haskins who rescued me then.

It's Dr. Haskins who's come to rescue me now.

I struggle with my hands, trying to reach up and touch her; to make sure she's real.

They won't budge and only serve to stir the stinging, healing waters that burble around my throat, my shoulders, the tips of my toes.

There is just enough water to cover most of me, just enough give on my binding to let me float near the top. My nose, mouth, eyes, and most of my ears are exposed to the briny chilled air above the Tank.

It's a little like floating in the lake as a kid, staring up at the summer sun and listening to the sounds of Labor Day as the other kids splash all around you, your mother on her oversized beach blanket, keeping the flies from your watermelon slice.

Dr. Haskins seems to be inspecting me or at least my progress. "How do you feel?" she whispers, almost tenderly. (Almost.)

I want to speak, to ask, to say many things, but

I can only croak, "Great."

I try to be a smart aleck, to raise my hand and give her a big, wet thumbs-up, but my wrists are tethered to the bottom of the tank.

She smiles, understanding, reaching out a soft hand to touch my forehead. "You know where you are?"

I go to answer, struggling on a large ball of phlegm.

"Nod or shake your head, Lily. Let's not rush this. You're not quite there yet."

I blink and wish I could still weep.

"You're in the Tank. You mustn't try to—"

"How long?" My voice sounds like I've returned from twelve straight rock concerts in a row, where I've screamed my lungs out and smoked a pack of cigarettes per song.

"Three days, and you're coming along nicely. There was tissue damage, of course, but none permanent. Your bones were fine. Your face too. Your ankles and hands will recover. Your legs got the worst of it, unfortunately, so there might be some scarring below the knee, but other than that, you should be okay."

I wish Dr. Haskins sounded more confident.

I wish I believed her.

I nod anyway, hearing the healing waters slosh around my ears, feeling my hair swirling around, beside, above my head. I must look like a water-logged Medusa.

The Tank is for recuperation of the most serious kind. It's filled with a secret recipe of healing powers handed down from the Council of Ancients. Some say the ingredients come straight from Transylvania; others say they come straight from a lab.

I don't care as long as it works, as long as I'm up and out of it before too long.

Vampires can heal without it in an emergency, but it's faster this way, with less scarring.

I concentrate and feel bubbles like seltzer fizzing around my deepest scars. It feels funny, almost like Sea-Monkeys are tickling me, and I can't help but think of those Scrubbing Bubbles commercials, where the smiling bubbles float over dirty shower tiles and leave them sparkling clean.

Is that what's happening down below?

Are the bubbles healing me, bringing my ravaged skin back to life?

I can't investigate because I'm fixed in place via cords tied to my wrists and ankles, elbows and knees, but I can feel the tingling sensation of healing happening.

I smile up at her. She's been waiting patiently.

How long has my mind been wandering, images

of Scrubbing Bubbles dancing on shower tiles?

"I have updates on your friends if you're ready."

I nod, the water roiling in my half-submerged ears.

"Although it's highly extraordinary, I have been given permission to harbor Tristan and Zander, who are both safe, by the way, here on campus."

"Here?" I can hear the excitement in my voice, the thought of Zander in the same building filling my chest with warm, fizzing bubbles of its own.

She seems almost impatient but smiles. "Where would you have me send them, dear?" she asks in a strained voice.

"Zander?"

At last she smiles knowingly. "Zander is fine, Lily. The other students are treating him very well, considering he tells everyone he meets how you saved his life. I would heal quickly, if I were you. The other girls have taken quite a shine to him. I must admit it's a tad . . . refreshing to have a human around."

I blush. "Not hurt?" I manage hoarsely.

"Not in the least," she explains. "If anything, he seems healthier than a mortal should be under the circumstances. I daresay he's auditing some of your old classes, Stake Sharpening 101, Fencing for Dummies, that kind of thing. From the looks of things, he's adapting quite well."

I grin, the tightness in my face keeping me from smiling outright, picturing Zander strutting through the halls, curls bouncing, surrounded by vampires, not even wincing at the sight. Not after what he's been through.

"Tristan?" I say, trying to sound emotionless but failing.

"Yes, well, he's become quite the know-it-all, as you might imagine, but he's blending in just the same. I suppose that's how it is when the Royals turn them. They think they're better than the rest of us. Anyway, I'm keeping him on a short leash."

I nod and say hopelessly, "Cara? Alice?"

She pauses, her face a blank mask.

I prepare for the worst. Images of Grover fill my mind, the sound of his head hitting the marble wall of the chapel, the blood smear, that big, proud, jovial chest releasing its final breath. At least Cara and Alice died quickly and won't have to suffer their many permanent wounds.

Finally she says, "The damage to their cellular structure was severe, as you know, but there was enough of their nervous systems left to build on. The Saviors always bring along a medical staff, of course, in case of these types of emergencies. They were able to retrieve enough raw material for . . . regeneration.

"Of course, the damage was too severe to bring them here, to the Tank. The Council of Ancients have a program, though. They call it the Restoration. It will help them recover fully. Eventually. It will take some time—weeks, maybe even months—but you'll have your Sisters back safe and sound."

I exhale loudly.

To hear they'll be here is a relief.

Well, somewhat.

"And will they be like before?"

"Yes, well, Zander told me how they were behaving, and I sensed from the intact fangs we recovered at the scene that they had been turned by a Royal. The Ancients assure me they will be as they were before they were turned, not after, so you have that to look forward to."

I close my eyes for quite some time, feeling the impact of her words, what they mean, flooding my body.

When I look up, her face is grim, and I wonder if I imagined what I've heard.

"That's the good news," she says. "Unfortunately, as soon as you're out of there in another couple of days, you'll have to pay a visit to the Council of Ancients."

I nod slowly. "Why?"

She pauses, then explains, "A Royal was killed and, although you didn't pull the trigger, we weren't informed that it was a Royal before we came in blasting. No one's blaming you, and we all appreciate the service you did for the good people of Ravens Roost and, of course, the students at Nightshade, but there will be . . . repercussions. Do you understand?"

I blink and offer a weak smile.

She does the same.

She looks behind her at someone or something, but since I can't move my head that far without the healing waters blurring my vision, I can't see what or whom. "If you promise to behave and not talk too much and not get too terribly excited, I have a visitor I think you'll very much enjoy seeing."

She nods, almost bows, and then clacks away on her heels.

I listen to her move, then feel a different presence replace her at my side.

I feel heat move through my body as Zander leans down and he pecks me on the forehead.

"Hey, sleepyhead," he says, his eyes clear, his skin supple, his dark eyebrows raised. "We've all been worried about you."

"Missed you." I sound hoarser than ever.

"Whoa there." He chuckles. "They didn't give you a sex change or anything while I was away, did they?"

"Away?"

He smiles, reddens, like maybe he wasn't supposed to say anything. "I had a word with the Council of Ancients."

Hmm, Dr. Haskins didn't say anything about *that* little field trip.

"Well, since I'm the only human to ever see this place, I guess they wanted to check me out before they agreed to let me hang awhile."

"You passed?"

"I'm here, aren't I?"

"For how long?"

"That's up to you."

I nod, then swallow a lump and say, very slowly, the words like daggers in my throat, "I'm . . . sorry . . . about . . . Grover. I . . . tried. I . . . really—"

"I know you did. I was there, remember? You were as helpless as I was. She was too strong."

His eyes water until he shakes his head, clearing the tears, like maybe he's cried too many already.

I can imagine him in his new dorm suite here at the Academy for the last three days, alone probably since who would want to room with a vampire when you're a human, and vice versa?

Those first few nights tossing, turning, thinking Grover might be there when he woke up, imagining the walls covered with *Star Wars* posters, models flying from the ceiling, then finding only white-washed walls, bars on the window, an empty second room, no Grover, no me, no anybody.

How lonely he must have been. How lonely he must be still.

Smiling, he sputters, "If I know Grover, he's up there telling Obi-Wan Kenobi a thing or two about lightsabers."

The thought obviously makes him happy, so I stop myself from reminding him fictional characters don't go to heaven.

Come to think of it, the thought makes *me* smile too.

I close my eyes.

When I look up, he looks worried.

"You okay, Lily?"

I nod. "Why?"

He smirks, "No reason. You just took a little trip on me. That's all."

I shake my head and frown. "How do I look?"

He grins. "Well, I wish I could say you were naked in there, but they had to go and cover you up on account of my visit. But what I can see looks good, Lily. Real good."

"Perv." I laugh, and it takes a lot of energy. I smile, close my eyes again, and when I come to he's looking away.

"You're tired," he says gently, leaning in. "I'll let you rest."

"Don't want to," I say, struggling to stay awake.

"Yeah, but you need to," he insists, almost paternally. "I'll see you soon, and we can catch up."

I close my eyes, and when I wake Zander is gone.

I close them again, giving in to the warm, healing waters, the messages my body is sending, the fizzy, fuzzy healing bubbles that scrub me clean.

If only they could get inside my body, dig around my heart, scour my brain, and erase the ugly images of Cara and Alice threatening me and the boys, of Grover's blood staining the chapel walls.

I blink and try to think of happier things.

Like, had I dreamed Zander's kiss on my forehead?

Or was he really here at the Academy?

And when would I be out of the Tank so I could kiss him for real?

CHAPTER 35

The vehicle cruises along a pedestrian highway. I am in the passenger seat, dressed comfortably in loose clothes to promote my healing: yoga pants a size too big, a soft peasant blouse even bigger, leather sandals. (Yecch.)

We've been on the road for hours, never stopping, never slowing, driving endlessly onward until at last Dr. Haskins pulls off the main highway and onto several rural roads, the twists and turns so frequent I wouldn't know where I was even if I weren't blindfolded.

"How do you feel?" she says, speaking for the first time in over an hour.

"Physically or emotionally?"

"Let's start with physically and go from there."

"I'm good. Strong."

"No more headaches, pains, strains?"

I shake my head, though I can't tell if she's looking at me. "I feel better than ever, actually."

"That's the idea."

I feel the car round another bend, and the sound of soft dirt on the tires turns to chugging gravel.

"The healing waters don't just fix you. They're supposed to make you better than before."

I smile.

She must be looking because she asks, "What?"

"Nothing. Well, it's like that old TV series. 'We can make her better, faster, stronger.' Remember?"

"*Bionic Woman.*"

I nod.

The car cruises to a halt, and I hear Dr. Haskins shift into park, gather what sounds like a purse, and slide her keys out of the ignition.

There is a slight pause. "You can take that off now."

I do and blink at the late afternoon light filtering through the heavily tinted windows.

"Wow." I'm looking at the architectural monstrosity in front of us.

"Indeed," she says, smiling.

This isn't a mansion so much as a palace, a place fit for kings, queens, and I suppose Ancients. Vampires who have been alive so long they know what it was like to ride horses to work, to see London pre-bridge, to visit Paris pre–Eiffel Tower, to walk in Washington pre–White House. You get my drift. Ancients.

The building is as long as a bus terminal and at least six stories high. The façade is dismal and gray and dotted with lead-paned windows full of maroon curtains.

It looks like an old English manor, but it's so much bigger. Like a giant tomb but so much prettier.

There is no one to greet us as Dr. Haskins opens her car door, or so it would appear.

The minute we get out of the car, however, gunmen emerge from a series of animal topiaries scattered along the long, curving drive.

They are large, pale men with identical long black hair and black fatigues. The uniforms are tight, but their many pockets make them look baggy. Epaulets are on the shoulders, and each soldier wears a black beret.

I smile, despite my grim surroundings, thinking of the bright pink beret Cara bought me the day I officially became a Sister.

The servicemen don't approach the car but

observe it warily, each standing in front of his appointed topiary: an elephant, a giraffe. Three more emerge from a family of gigantic ducks.

"Sentries," Dr. Haskins says as we approach the mansion's huge front doors. "They're like the personal guard for the Ancients."

I nod.

I've heard of the Ancients and, to a lesser extent, the Sentries for years but never actually seen one.

Until now.

The closer we get to the door, the closer the Sentries get to us.

Dr. Haskins reaches for the handle, and a Sentry moves to stand in front of her.

"IDs," he says bluntly, fangs out, skin so pale and white it might as well be made from milk.

We whip out our Vampire Citizen IDs like driver's licenses for the living dead, featuring not our pictures but samples of our DNA. He scans them with a device no bigger than a cell phone, obviously likes what he sees, and opens the door. "After you."

"Now what?"

Half the Sentries lead us through the longest hall I've ever seen.

I'm talking, the entirety of Nightshade Conservatory for Exceptional Boys and Girls could fit in this entryway.

"Now," she says grimly, "we pay the piper."

CHAPTER 36

Six Ancients are gathered in a semicircle of antique chairs in the middle of a gargantuan room that makes the entrance hall look like a guest bathroom. I want to shout just to hear the echo off the walls. On each of their heads, the hair is either completely gone or silky white and sparse, the skin so paper thin and pale you can almost see through it to the flat, black veins dead and useless beneath.

Their eyes are shrunken and opaque, so white they might all have cataracts, like my great-grandmother did a few months after she moved into the nursing home in Florida.

Their fangs are permanently out, like those

sports cars with pop-up headlights that stop going down over the years. They are yellowed by time and perhaps use.

The Council of Ancients are dressed all in white. White linen, to be precise. The clothes hang on them like hand-me-downs on a third grader. Drawstring pants, pirate-type shirts with ties at the neck and puffy sleeves, slip-on shoes like your great-grandfather might wear.

They sit in high-backed chairs with velvet, padded seats.

Next to each Ancient is a cane with a silver tip. Behind each chair is a black-clad Sentry standing at the ready, uniform stiff, spine stiffer, beret like a black cherry on top of an evil sundae.

Two chairs are aligned in front of the Ancients. They are smaller than the chairs the Ancients sit in but no less formal.

Four Sentries, their guns at the ready, guide us to our seats.

They remain at attention long after Dr. Haskins and I sit.

The hall is quiet, deathly so.

The way my chair creaks when I shift my weight sounds like fireworks on the Fourth of July.

The ceiling must stretch two or three stories high, with great, iron chandeliers hanging on chains long enough to lasso a bull . . . even if that bull lived in the next county. Hundreds of white candles flicker in the snappy, damp breeze filling the room, though the big bare windows lining the wall are closed.

No one speaks for quite some time.

Dr. Haskins, for one, is particularly subdued.

I'm so used to seeing her in charge of the Academy, her spine straight, her glasses in place, her hair up, her clipboard clutched, it's odd and the slightest bit unsettling to see her looking so meek in the chair next to mine.

She stares ahead at some point directly over the Ancients' heads.

I admit there is much to look at.

Huge tapestries billow down, bursting with violent hunting scenes in vivid splashes of color.

There are old white Englishmen on big white horses hunting small orange foxes in the wild green forest, gray wolves hunting white sheep in the tan fields, even an enormous black bear hunting salmon in a rushing blue stream. All feature blood, buckets of it.

I can't tell which is worse, staring at the endless

violent depictions or the wizened faces of the Ancients beneath them.

Time passes. Who knows how much? I get the feeling time isn't quite the same for vampires this old. No clock ticks, no feet move, no chair legs scrape against the slate floor. There's only the steady flickering of candles and the endless passage of time.

A firm voice issues from one of the Ancients sitting in the middle. "Dr. Haskins, kneel before the Ancients to plead your case."

"Master," she says, her voice subdued and oddly reverent. She stands, quickly crouches, then kneels. "I come here today with great sorrow in my heart, for I readily confess that I have broken one of the Ancient laws."

"Which law did you break?" another Ancient from the end of the row says, his lips barely moving.

"Master, I have committed that great sin known as ignorance."

"Explain yourself," says another Ancient.

"My student here was sent to stop an infestation. I—"

"We know the particulars," an Ancient bellows. "What was thy part in all this?"

"Master, I killed a Royal."

There is no gasp, no sound of shock or outrage, only a murmuring among the six pale faces.

A clear voice interrupts. "Go on."

"It was no one's fault, Master. Lily here called for backup. I provided it. There was no time for her to relay to me that the target was a Royal. I shot her, sirs, through the heart."

"You know the penalty for killing a Royal?" they ask.

"Of course." She gasps.

I want to reach down and pick her up and run out of this place. I don't, of course, but I want to.

"And are you prepared to accept that penalty, Dr. Haskins?"

The slightest pause. "Yes, Master."

I close my eyes out of fear, but a rippling in the air forces me to open them.

An Ancient stands before us, right next to Dr. Haskins.

"Rise, Dr. Haskins, and receive your punishment."

On trembling knees my headmistress rises, formally greeting the Ancient with a dry kiss upon each hand.

He says quietly, "Your punishment, Dr. Haskins, is to learn the error of your ways. Even if it takes you all eternity to do so. To make the Afterlife Academy better than it was, so this kind of mistake never happens again. We don't condone what the Royal known as Bianca was doing, nor can we condone killing a Royal without punishment. From now until we decree the Sisterhood disbanded, I charge you with making the program the best it can be."

She bows and quickly leaves the room.

The Ancient turns to me. His face is grim, but his eyes are gentle. "Identify yourself."

"Lily Fielding." My voice sounds like its old self again. Okay, maybe a bit more trembly than usual, but you sit in front of a thousand-year-old vampire and see how steady your nerves are.

He nods weakly and takes Dr. Haskins' chair, moving it slightly so we can see each other.

"What is your crime, Lily Fielding?"

"I-I-I was the reason Dr. Haskins killed a Royal, sir."

"Indeed, you were." His hands look like a skeleton's as he rests them on his baggy linen pants. "However, you also did us a great service by not allowing Nightshade to be infested."

I open my mouth to agree, but it seems in bad form, so I close it again.

"Am I to understand that you also alerted a human to your true existence?"

I nod, looking him in the white, gauzy eyes. "Two, actually, but one got turned into a vampire, so . . ."

He stands, gently touching my arm and bringing me with him.

"Lily Fielding, this Council sentences you to a lifetime as a Sister. You shall continue saving young girls from rogues who would seduce them for their own means. You will not, alas, become a Savior. What's more, you will be forever bound to this mortal in your charge. This, this . . . Zander . . . person. You told him our secrets. Therefore, he is your responsibility. Do you understand? If he helps us, you reap the rewards. If he harms us, you will take the blame."

I nod, since he seems to be waiting for a response.

"It is a great responsibility to have someone's life in your hands. Let us hope you take it seriously and show him that not all vampires are bad."

I nod again, and he drifts slowly back to the Council.

"Go, Lily." His voice echoes as clearly, as closely, as if he were still standing in front of me. "Go and accept your punishment, and make the Council proud."

The Sentries lead me from the great hall, a walk that seems to take many long hours.

A part of me is wistful. Another part is hopeful

that in this new world I can play a role to help humans and vampires understand one another.

Before the great doors open, I turn to cast my gaze on the Ancients once more. They have already left the room, their chairs as silent and empty as the sentence they have imposed.

I turn toward the heavy doors, a Sentry on each side, and face my future.

CHAPTER 37

The Healing Room is bleak and quiet and staffed by vampires so old and neglected they might as well be zombies. With fangs. And doctor's scrubs. And more old man slippers (the Ancients must get a discount).

Alice and Cara lie on marble slabs next to each other, naked except for muslin cloths covering them from chest to midthigh.

There are no healing waters, no mineral baths.

Here the Healers attend to them 24-7, rubbing them constantly with sponges and solutions, massaging their skin with creams and lotions, feeding them blood through an IV tube in each wrist, literally nursing them to health.

They don't look good.

Cara's skin is no longer a beautiful, sexy mocha but an ashy gray. That is, where she's not scarred like a burn victim. Her head is not bald, exactly, but gone are her beautiful cornrows and long, delicate lashes.

I cringe to see her this way, but I have to admit she looks better than the last time I saw her.

They've come so far, from rib cages and barely attached femurs to living flesh and bone. Ugly and rough as it is, it's amazing.

Alice is in worse shape, her skin mottled and likewise gray, her calves covered in flesh so thin it's like that see-through half guy in anatomy class, the one whose liver and lungs you take out and put back in wrong (at least I always do).

She shakes like she's having a bad dream, and when I go to brush her forehead softly, it's almost on fire.

They make no noise.

I tremble.

Dr. Haskins puts an arm around my shoulder and steers me out of the room.

"They'll be fine, Lily. Another few weeks you'll forget all about what you saw."

"I'll never forget what I saw. Never."

"Good," she says, back to headmistress mode. "Let's hope not. You heard your sentence?"

"I did."

We are walking down the great hall, toward the main entrance, no longer flanked by Sentries now that our private visit is over.

"Then you know there is no more chance of your becoming a Savior."

"I know."

"There is a silver lining." She pauses. "As permanent headmistress of the Afterlife Academy for the Exceptionally Dark Arts, I would like to make you permanent First Sister."

I stop, twist one of my soft shoes on the varnished floor. "Do you mean it?"

She halts. "Of course I do."

I smile, then frown. "Oh, I guess it only makes sense, considering the shape Alice and Cara are in."

She shakes her head. "I said permanent First Sister, Lily. This has nothing to do with the shape Alice and Cara are in. You may not believe this, but I actually do work in that office of mine. Part of my work is to find out what happens on your missions. Since Alice and Cara were obviously out of commission and you were in the Tank, I took it upon myself to interview the only living witnesses to your latest mission."

"You mean Zander?"

"And Tristan. Both assured me you acted like a consummate professional, calmly, rationally keeping things together. Tristan was particularly impressed with how, even when you could have escaped, you chose to face certain death to rescue Zander. And, of course, Zander had nothing but positive things to say about you. I would say that's First Sister material, wouldn't you?"

I shake my head. "I only did what you trained me to do, which is to support my First and Second Sisters. It wasn't their fault what happened. You weren't there. You didn't see Bianca in her prime. She was all-powerful. She lured them away, tricked them. Otherwise they would have never turned on me like they—"

But I can tell she already knows all this.

She pats my hand and says, "Be that as it may, on this mission you were the only one to act like a First Sister, and so shall it be."

I nod, then allow the beginnings of a smile to lift the corners of my lips. "Okay"—I shrug—"if you insist." Inside I'm cheering, leaping, yelping, clicking my heels like a leprechaun who's finally found his pot of gold.

"That's not all," she says, walking again toward the grand front doors. "I would like to propose we make a few other changes to the Sisterhood of Dangerous Girlfriends."

"Really? Like what?"

"Well, for one, I'd like to put your friends Tristan and Zander to good use."

"How would that work?" I ask, picturing them in pink berets. "I mean, we're Sisters, right?"

"I'd like to send you, all five of you, as a team on your next assignment. I think it would be helpful in the future to have boys in the Sisterhood, in case, for instance, you run up against another Vampress."

"Sounds good," I say, wondering how Tristan and Zander will feel about being called Sisters.

"Might mean a name change."

"No way." I gasp. "You can't stop calling us Sisters because I screwed up one assignment."

Nearly to the front door, she chuckles dryly. "Your call, of course, but you might want to check with your Brothers first."

"Didn't you hear? I'm permanent First Sister. I

don't have to check with nobody for nothin'."

She laughs.

I stop her before opening the door. "Dr. Haskins?"

"Yes?"

I look around, see no Sentries gawking, and ask, "What *is* the punishment for killing a Royal?"

She nods grimly, looks around, and says very quietly, "Exile."

"Exile? That's it? I thought they'd, like, kill you or something."

"Oh, Lily, exile is worse than death. It's like being a wild animal."

I look at Dr. Haskins' modern glasses, her well-coiffed hair, her sleek suit and shiny heels, and I see how exile could be worse than death to a woman like her. "Well, then, here's to not being exiled."

She smiles and pulls something out of her jacket pocket. "One last tiny detail," she says, holding up the blindfold for our long trip home to the Academy.

EPILOGUE

Zander enters the Simulation House, his stakes up and at the ready, his long, curly locks shoved tight under a black watch cap. (Bummer.)

He looks sleek and athletic in his black track suit and sneakers.

As we've been practicing every day since they let me out of the Tank, he pivots in three directions to clear the foyer: front, back, side.

I mouth *good boy* to the glowing security monitor.

He walks carefully but not slowly into the living room.

"So far so good." Dr. Haskins' expression is pinched.

"*Good* being the operative word," says Tristan,

looking stiff and polished in his charcoal slacks and dress shirt, unbuttoned, his broad chest marble pale and hairless underneath. He peers from Zander on the security monitor to me looking down at it, cheering him on silently with crossed fingers (on each hand).

"Pathetic," he whispers, seeing my cheerleader-like enthusiasm.

I stick out my tongue.

Dr. Haskins scores Zander on the paper held in her see-through clipboard.

I regard Tristan critically. (Okay, so I can't help it!) He has matured beyond his years in his short time at the Academy, becoming a dominant force and a likely candidate for the Saviors at some point in the near future. That is, if as permanent First Sister I ever choose to let him out of the Sisterhood.

I keep my distance, mostly because Zander occupies all my time but also because I've grown wary of Tristan's sleek, almost magnetic good looks and his predatory nature.

Although he's appealing on paper, excelling in his coursework, rising to the top of his fencing and stake-wielding classes, he still wavers between good and evil like he did at Nightshade.

I'll never be able to forget, let alone forgive, the

sight of his bloody leg disappearing up into the air duct when we needed him most.

I don't want to trust him, but I have to.

He and Zander share a love-hate relationship but a relationship nonetheless. Zander thinks he's a stuck-up snob. Tristan agrees but hates Zander's humanity.

I don't know if it's the Royal blood or simply the vampire blood running through his veins that makes Tristan prejudiced against mortals. Where once he and Zander shared a cordial relationship based on a mutual past at Nightshade, now they are increasingly competitive.

I expect it from Tristan, with his spoiled upbringing and Royal blood, but it's surprising to see in Zander.

"Ouch," he says, bringing me back to reality—and hard. Through the monitor I see Zander pat a stake that's entered the wall about two inches, maybe less, above his head.

"Good reflexes on this one," Dr. Haskins says.

Tristan rolls his eyes.

I stifle a smile.

Good for you, Zander.

Zander doesn't let the booby trap stop him but instead doubles his efforts to clear the ruined dining room.

The monitor switches perspective. Zander is at the foot of the stairs. Our view comes from a security camera mounted in the ceiling at the top of the stairs.

He takes the first, tentative step. He crouches low, like I taught him, leaning on the handrail to avoid putting much pressure on the stairs themselves. He leaps deftly to avoid one booby trap, only to land on a second. The stake passes centimeters from his thigh.

"Ouch," Tristan says, finger combing his vampirific hair. "A few inches higher and you'd have another Sister for your little club."

I ignore him, as does Dr. Haskins.

Meanwhile Zander rushes up the stairs.

I can't help but notice how much he too has changed during his brief stay at the Academy. Although he is still very much human, the one and only here at the Academy, he seems somewhat more than human.

The geeky but adorable softness he had at Nightshade is gone, replaced by a more muscular appearance. Must be all those late-night training sessions I put him through.

And if you think I'm just being naughty, we actually do train, thank you very much.

You know, mostly.

He looks grimmer as well. Perhaps it's because unlike most humans, who only fantasize about Hollywood vampires, he knows that real monsters exist. That they look like you and me. Well, more like me. And that friends who die—good friends, real friends—don't come back like at the end of Hollywood B movies.

But it's more than that.

Dr. Haskins glances at me. I think she sees it too.

She warned me once I got out of the Tank that while Zander and I could "dabble in romantic notions," as she so sensibly put it, we could never "consummate" our love.

We haven't, of course.

Not yet anyway, but that hasn't stopped us from swapping spit on a regular basis.

And therein is the rub.

When I get excited at the taste of Zander's lips, when my blood boils with the touch of his fingertips on my shoulder blades, my fangs tend to protrude. From time to time I nick him: his tongue, his gums, the inside of his cheeks. And once, only once, his neck.

He calls it fang play, but I feel horrible each time it happens. Truly, really horrible, and not only because I'm sure it hurts but because I think it's gradually . . . changing him.

My saliva—gross, I know, but stay with me here—is also somewhat special.

Vampires don't merely suck blood. We also secrete.

When our fangs go in, even a little, out comes a special venom through our saliva which thins the blood of our victims.

It's easier, quicker to consume thinner blood. You know, the same way you let your milk shake melt a bit so it comes up the straw when you're driving home, that big bag of burgers and fries riding shotgun.

Naturally, some of the saliva contains vampire DNA, and I think Zander here has had his fair share in the last few weeks. Maybe even more than his fair share, if you know what I mean.

Not that it means much in the grand scheme of things. I'd still have to turn him to make it official, but I can tell he's changing, morphing into something more than human but not quite vampire.

I kind of like that.

I think he secretly does too.

He's in the guest room now. One more room to go.

I stare at the big digital clock on the wall. Still four minutes left.

"Is it just me," Tristan says, "or is he getting faster every time we do this?" He adds, "Not fast enough"—it wouldn't be Tristan if he gave an actual compliment, especially to a human—"but faster."

"We train every night after school," I insist, forgetting Tristan has a way of turning everything innocent into something not so innocent, at least when it comes to Zander and me.

"Yeah, the same way porn stars train."

"Silence," Dr. Haskins says. "He's in the master bedroom. It's do or die time. I do hope he's up for it."

Zander crouches and moves through the room, his cap slightly askew, a tear in his track suit where the last stake barely missed.

Something catches my eye: a square of carpet, not like all the others, as big as a hamburger patty, maybe even smaller. Instinctively I know it hides a trap.

I'm hovering over the monitor, wanting to shout, "Look out, Zander. Watch out, honey. It's a trap!"

He steps on it, feels the hiss, and leaps forward, but the stake catches the sole of his shoe and dumps him, face-first, into the carpet.

It looks like it hurts, but he rolls over, sits up, and seems okay. He stands and checks the bottom of his shoe, which is missing a chunk of rubber sole.

He shakes his head and gets to work.

With eighty-seven seconds to spare, Zander reaches the square button on the wall, which signifies he's cleared all six rooms, and pushes it soundly.

Immediately the curtains part, the glass door hisses, and Dr. Haskins steps out of the office and into the Simulation room.

Once she's through it, the door hisses shut behind her.

I pace her office.

They confer.

Tristan looks on edge, as if he's bet money on a horse race with a photo finish and is waiting for the official to tell him who's won so he can collect or get out of Dodge.

Zander walks through the door and immediately reaches for my hand. I let him lead me into the hall and, with nowhere else to go, Tristan dutifully follows.

"So," I say, racing to keep up with his frantic pace, "do tell. What'd she say?"

Zander yanks off his ski cap and scratches his long, curly hair. "She said I beat Tristan's time by seven whole seconds."

"Impossible," Tristan says, but I detect the smallest trace of pride in his voice.

Zander rushes ahead to the cafeteria, calling out over his shoulder, "Come on. I'm starved!"

"I don't know why he's in such a hurry." Tristan sighs. "The only thing on the menu is blood."

Zander is already inside the cafeteria, the doors still swinging in his wake.

I grab Tristan's arm, slowing him down in the hallway, and ask, "Why are you so hard on him? He's only a kid. A human kid. Can't you see he looks up to you?"

He grits his teeth. "What do *you* see in him, Lily? He's just a . . . a mortal."

"I like him no matter what he is. Why can't you?"

"I should think you'd know." He fiddles with his wide disco collar.

"I do know, Tristan, okay? I'm not blind. But what we had was one kiss. And I wasn't the one who ruined it. Yes, I felt something for you, but—"

"Felt?" He reaches for my arm.

I let him. "Feel, felt, what's the difference? I'm with Zander. It happened. I'm happy. Why can't you let me be happy?"

"Is that what you really want?"

"Is that so hard to believe?"

He releases me.

I take two steps closer to the cafeteria.

"Things change." He turns around and walks away. "I'll be here when they do."

"If they do," I shout at his back, hoping I sound convincing.

He waves over his shoulder, a dismissive gesture.

I'm so mad I could toss a stake at one of his strutting butt cheeks this very minute.

I control myself and head toward the cafeteria. I hear cheers and hustle through the door to see what's happening.

Two wheelchair-bound vampires blow party horns and toss confetti into the air with their bandaged hands. There is a small cake on one of the empty cafeteria tables with a single candle burning in its center in honor of Zander making it through Simulation House.

Zander bends to gently peck Alice's and Cara's cheeks.

He blows out the candle and offers cake to the vampires, who easily turn it down.

Cara smiles, though weakly. Her skin is coming along nicely, though bandages still cover her knees, ankles, elbows, and wrists, joints where the healing process takes the longest.

I bend to kiss her nearly bald head.

"Hey, you." Her voice is scratchy. Her vocal cords are still threading together while the healing process comes to completion.

"What's the verdict?" I sit on the edge of a cafeteria table.

Zander playfully tries to get Alice to eat a slice of cake.

She sees me, stops laughing for a moment. I nod at Alice and she turns back to Zander; I can't tell if she's satisfied or smug. I guess, with her, I'll never know.

"Dr. Haskins says I should be good to go by the end of the month."

I pat her bandaged knee. "Still Second Sister?"

She shoots a competitive look at Alice and nods. "For now."

"And you?" I ask, wagging a finger at Alice.

She scratches the bandage over her healing scalp. "A few more weeks and I'll be giving you and Cara a run for your money."

I smile.

It feels weird, being First Sister, knowing Alice resents it and Cara maybe disagrees with it.

It is what it is, and this time there's nothing

Alice or Cara can do about it.

Despite their actions at Nightshade, I still love my Sisters. I'm thankful Dr. Haskins had the presence of mind to ship what was left of their bodies to the Healing Center. And I'm glad they returned here a few days ago.

Cara looks at the silent cafeteria door. The missing member of our group has yet to materialize.

"Tristan's not coming?" she says quietly, not wanting to announce the fact to Zander.

I shrug. "He says he's feeling threatened."

"Uh-huh. What'd I tell you about bringing your work home with you? It never ends well."

"Where was he supposed to go?" I ask.

"You know," Cara adds, "since you've already got your hands full with Zander, why don't you give me a shot at your sloppy seconds?"

"Be my guest."

I look up to find Zander cluelessly helping himself to another slice of cake a few feet away.

Alice, sensing blood in the water, wheels herself over with bandaged hands, wincing slightly. "What am I missing?"

Cara sends me a *shut up* vibe, but I ignore her. This gossip is too spicy to resist. "Oh, nothing. Cara here was just putting in an order for one plate of Tristan to go."

"Not if I get to him first," Alice says, and I'm sure she's serious.

Trouble is, so is Cara. "Come on, Alice. You've already dated half the guys here. Why don't you give a Sister a break?"

"With a hunk like that," Alice says, "the only thing he's breaking is hearts."

"Cheesy," I say.

Cara nods. "So cheesy."

"Hey, what can I say? He inspires the poet in me."

Cara looks glum. "Yeah, well, right now the only one inspiring him is Lily, and she won't have anything to do with him."

"I didn't say that," I whisper. "I just . . . we have a history and not a good one. I'm not ready to put that behind me yet."

"Girl," Alice says, rolling her eyes, "I'd put that behind me any day of the week!"

"Gross." Cara laughs.

"You know what I mean, Alice."

Just like that, Zander is back, sucking his frosting-covered thumbs, a spot of blue icing on his thick, human lips.

"Who we talking about?" he says.

But I know he's far from a fool.

"We have presents!" Alice hands him a small wrapped box, about the size of a CD.

Cara hands him one too. It's longer and shaped like, well, shaped like what it is.

He opens Cara's first, revealing his very own monogrammed stake. *Zander* is branded into the side.

"Now we each have one," Cara says.

He makes an *ahhhh* face before ripping into Alice's. It's a bright pink beret. He looks at Alice and Cara, who, with some difficulty, are putting their own pink berets on their mostly bald heads.

They turn to me, and mine is already on. Hey, a First Sister always comes prepared!

"Whoa," Zander says, reluctantly pulling his hat onto his head. "Tristan and I were discussing this, and there's no reason we can't rename the group."

"To what?" Cara says.

"I dunno. We were thinking something along the lines of the Brotherhood of Badass Boyfriends or something. Waddya think? Alice? Cara? Work with me here."

Alice and Cara wisely take the matter into consideration, conferring in their old talkative way.

Zander wanders, and I walk alongside him. His beret is cockeyed atop those delectable curls. Sometimes I miss the boy Zander was, even as I'm lusting for the man he has become.

He grins, hands behind his back. "You ready for a little competition?"

"You ready to be a Sister?" I tease.

"Only if it means spending more time with you." He bats his eyelashes.

"That's sweet," I say, slugging his shoulder.

"Want something really sweet?" he says, bringing his finger around. It's covered in frosting.

"Uhhm, I would love nothing more than to lick that finger clean, Zander, but not here." I make a scrunchy face at Cara and Alice to prove my point.

"Come on." He pushes the finger closer to my face. "No one's watching."

"You walked through that grimy Simulation House. You know how many germs are in there?"

"You're a vampire, Lily. You can't die."

"Ah, but you can, and that's *exactly* what will happen if you keep shoving that nasty finger in my face."

He keeps pushing it, pushing it, until I bend his arm behind his back.

And that is where Cara catches us, snapping her digital camera, smiling, the Sisterhood complete and with a couple new Brothers to boot.

Also from
Rusty Fischer
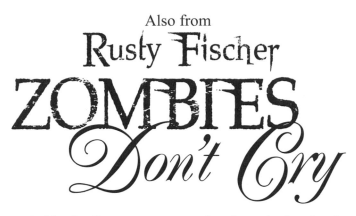
ZOMBIES
Don't Cry

Maddy Swift is just a normal girl—a high school junior surviving class with her best friend and hoping the yummy new kid, Stamp, will ask her out. When he finally does, her whole life changes.

Sneaking out to meet Stamp at a party one rainy night, Maddy is struck by lightning. After awakening, she feels lucky to be alive. Over time, however, Maddy realizes that she's become the thing she and everyone else fear most: the living dead.

With no heartbeat and no breath in her lungs, Maddy must learn how to survive as a zombie. Turns out there's a lot more to it than shuffling around 24/7 growling, "Brains." Needing an afterlife makeover is only the beginning of her problems. As Barracuda Bay High faces zombie Armageddon, Maddy must summon all of her strength to protect what matters most—just as soon as she figures out exactly what that is.

ISBN# 9781605423821
US $9.95 / CDN $11.95
Trade Paperback / Young Adult Fiction
Available Now
http://zombiesdontblog.blogspot.com

Look for These Upcoming Titles
by Rusty Fischer!

- Afterlife Academy-2013
- Vampire Book of the Month Club-2014

Want to read more from Rusty?
Visit Zombies Don't Blog at
http://zombiesdontblog.blogspot.com

Or find him on Facebook and Twitter

MEDALLION

P   R   E   S   S

Be in the know on the latest
Medallion Press news by becoming a
Medallion Press Insider!

<u>As an Insider you'll receive:</u>

• Our FREE expanded monthly newsletter,
giving you more insight into Medallion Press

• Advanced press releases and breaking news

• Greater access to all of your favorite
Medallion authors

Joining is easy. Just visit our website at
<u>www.medallionpress.com</u> and click on the
Medallion Press Insider tab.

m e d a l l i o n p r e s s . c o m

MEDALLION

P R E S S

Want to know what's going on with
your favorite author or what new releases
are coming from Medallion Press?

Now you can receive breaking news,
updates, and more from Medallion Press
straight to your cell phone, e-mail, instant
messenger, or Facebook!

Sign up now at www.twitter.com/MedallionPress
to stay on top of all the happenings in and
around Medallion Press.

For more information
about other great titles from
Medallion Press, visit
m e d a l l i o n p r e s s . c o m